MW01251885

VAMPIRES, ZOMBIES AND
GHOSTS
VOLUME TWO

Read on the Run
Anthology

Margery Bayne

Gina Burgess

Dianna Duncan

Laurie Axinn Gienapp

Jude-Marie Green

Liam Hogan

Geri Leen

Jessica Lévai

Laird Long

R. J. Meldrum

Michael Penncavage

C. M. Saunders

Scott Savino

Ginny Swart

Catherine Valenti

Desmond Warzel

Vampires, Zombies and Ghosts, Volume 2

Copyright © 2019 by Smoking Pen Press, LLC

Edited by Catherine Valenti and Laurie Gienapp

Cover design by Elle J. Rossi http://www.EvernightDesigns.com

Smoking Pen Press
PO Box 190835
Boise, ID 83719
www.smokingpenpress.com
ISBN-13:9781944289164
First Edition: August 2019

COPYRIGHT NOTICES

Bonus Material:

TABLE OF CONTENTS

INTRODUCTION   7

ELEVENSES   8
Liam Hogan

THE FINAL BITE   17
Laurie Axinn Gienapp

AT WIT'S END   27
Catherine Valenti

A GOOD BOY   47
Desmond Warzel

THE SPREE   58
Jessica Lévai

RUN FOR THE ROSES   65
Gerri Leen

SMITTEN   71
Ginny Swart

THE LAY OF THE LAND   80
Jude-Marie Green

DOWN THE ROAD   93
C. M. Saunders

ASPIRIN   103
SCOTT SAVINO

GHOMESTIC   109
LAIRD LONG

THROUGH THE GLASS DARKLY   119
MARGERY BAYNE

TRICK OR TREAT   138
DIANNA DUNCAN

ALWAYS PARIS   144
R. J. MELDRUM

THE HIT   160
MICHAEL PENNCAVAGE

GIMLET   168
GINA BURGESS

BONUS MATERIAL
RAGE   179
CATHERINE VALENTI

HELL OF A DAY   199
LAURIE AXINN GIENAPP

OTHER TITLES PUBLISHED BY SMOKING PEN PRESS   204

INTRODUCTION

We asked for stories about vampires, zombies, ghosts and other supernatural creatures, and that's what we received. In fact, we received so many—and so many that were so good, that we've had to divide them into two volumes in order to give you a Read on the Run.

As in Volume 1, this volume has a lot of ghost stories, as well as some vampire stories and zombie stories. Also just as in Volume 1, these are not your stereotypical ghosts, vampires, and zombies… they are unique, and have their own twist.

In addition to those stories, we have some extras. We offer you a demon, a cupid, a werewolf, and even a mermaid.

And, as a bonus, we've included two extra stories that have appeared in previous titles in the Read on the Run series.

As always, each story in the Read on the Run series of anthologies is short, to suit your busy lifestyle.

ELEVENSES

Liam Hogan

Editor's Note: Elevenses *is a British reference to a short break for light refreshments, usually with tea or coffee, taken about eleven o'clock in the morning.*

TICK, TOCK; REPETITION, routine; the things we cling to at the bookends of our lives; from the toddler watching the same videos over and over until the parents pray, or perhaps arrange, for a malfunction, to the old age pensioner sitting in a retirement home fretting because her normally punctual eleven o'clock tea is a quarter-hour late.

I'd ignored the morning's commotion, the usual noises of mayhem and distress. Berrylands is not the quietest of places at the best of times and if you'd been here as long as I had, you'd get used to the incoherent screams of frustration as Mrs Woods and her helper search once again for her missing upper dentures. Perhaps I'd been unwise to turn a deaf ear. Perhaps the noises—the thuds, the

8

crashes, the animal howls—and my missing cup of under-brewed, over-milked lukewarm tea were somehow connected.

Still, it's quiet now. Even the usual car alarms and police sirens from the busy London street outside have fallen silent. I wonder if I've been forgotten. Or is this punishment for flipping Ms Prenderghast—the thickset and sullen manager of this mouldering nursing home—the bird? I can't even remember why I'd done so, but this, I am quite sure, is not a sign of senility. This is having too many reasons to recall which particular offence might have sent me over the edge.

And anyway, aren't we old folk allowed to misbehave? Doesn't my grey hair, wrinkled features and Zimmer frame give me free rein to say and do as I feel?

I don't think Ms Prenderghast would agree. I'm sure she'd be far happier if we were all permanently drugged to the eyeballs, and not on ecstasy, either.

Oh, that's really rather clever. Wasn't ecstasy originally invented as a cure for dementia? I must tell Muriel that. Unless it was LSD? Or something else altogether? I was born a little too early for all that stuff, though it pays, I think, to drop the odd comment into the conversation. Stops them thinking I'm some sort of fossil. Stops them forgetting about me.

The little mantel clock with its fat green arms shows twenty-five past, and still no tea. Definitely, incontrovertibly, late. Very well then, it is time to sally forth. I will make my own blasted cuppa! At least I'll get the colour right, and it will be scaldingly hot, just how I like it.

I creak as I push myself upright, click and pop as I pull the Zimmer towards me. I am serenaded by my very own orchestra of arthritic and aging joints. Such is old age. I shuffle my way to the door.

Which is locked.

They've never gone this far before, this is more than willful neglect. As I hover in my crouched forward position, I imagine smuggling a letter out to the local newspaper. I can see it now: social services raiding the home, finding me frail but stoic, the reporter breaking down in tears as I describe my distressing plight, Ms Prenderghast taken away in chains, a blanket thrown over her bovine features.

Though come to think of it, didn't the local paper close down fifteen years ago? Perhaps I should tweet it instead:

> *Hashtag SOS. Elderly lady imprisoned in Berrylands nursing home. May not survive the night. Send help, urgent! P.S. Bring a thermos of hot tea.*

Like I said, I wouldn't want them to think I'm a fossil.

How many followers did I have last time I checked? Two, I think. Derek and some guy from Zimbabwe who claims I hold the key to our mutual fortune. I somehow doubt he will be coming to my rescue. But blast it, this daydreaming isn't getting me anywhere. I drag the Zimmer and my own protesting frame over to the patio door that leads onto the little courtyard and try the handle. NOT locked! This is one pensioner they can't keep down!

I exit my room, ignore the other curtained bedrooms and head straight for the double-doors to the day lounge. Stupid bloody name for a room, that. It's not as if we have a night lounge, though maybe we should. Soft lights, cocktails, maybe even a piano. Now *that* would be a way to run a home.

I slide the glass-paned door back and see my first glimpse of a human since Jennie brought me my breakfast at around eight. And Jennie hardly counts, she's not exactly the chatty sort and this morning she was even worse than usual; distracted, jittery, must have asked me at least three times if I'd taken my meds.

From the pink cardie it looks like it's Silvia. Though what she's doing on the floor, I can't imagine, she's probably dropped a Murray Mint or something. She looks up through bloodshot eyes as I call her name, her face contorted, a ragged, oozing wound reaching from one cheek all the way down to the little silver clasp at her throat, a glimpse of something white behind the red, and that's when I realise that she doesn't really count as human either. Not anymore.

She snarls, and starts towards me, and in an instant it's only the Zimmer keeping her false teeth and her nicotine stained hands at bay. I twist the frame sideways, spilling her to the floor, and as she tumbles I lift the Zimmer and bring it down sharpish on the hip that has been on the NHS waiting list for some eighteen months now. She

11

howls and glares at me, but this time stays down, one hand clutching at her side as I totter past, *sans* Zimmer, into the hallway.

Truth is, I don't really need it—the Zimmer—not most days, anyway. But when you're the archetypal little old lady competing for corridor space with walking sticks, wheelchairs, and the occasional gurney, a Zimmer gives you a certain intransigence, an uncompromising width that demands and gets respect.

Though I do feel a little naked without it, especially as I turn the corner and come face to face with a similarly zombified Muriel. Which is a horrific shock to the system and a dirty rotten shame to boot, because at my age cribbage partners who still have their marbles intact are a rare breed indeed. I think she's as surprised to see me as I am her, and I dodge past before she manages more than a guttural groan. I don't tell her my quip about Ms Prenderghast feeding us ecstasy, I kind of think it would be wasted on Muriel as she seems to be missing both of her ears.

I'm beginning to fear the worst, and half think about returning to safety, but I'd have to go past Silvia and Muriel on my way back and by now I'm marginally closer to the kitchen than my room. I wish I had my cell phone with me though, much as the damn thing baffles the heck out of me. I'd call my nephew, Derek, and ask to speak to his nine-year-old son, Alfie. Last Christmas—the same Christmas Derek gifted me his reconditioned phone while trying to hide his brand-spanking-new one—Alfie shoved an Xbox controller into my hands and instructed me in the fine art of killing zombies. "Shoot them in the head, Nan!" he'd hollered as his parents had prepared dinner.

I wonder where the nearest gun shop is? It hadn't seemed particularly difficult on the screen, even for an old duffer like me, and I kind of liked the colourful way the zombie heads exploded when I shot them right.

Not quite as colourful or realistic as Jennie's head which I pass a good few metres before I have to pick my way over her fallen body. She's got a bunch of keys clutched in her hand—room keys. I'd guess it was she who locked me in. Probably saved my life, or what little I have left of it. If this is the end of the world and if the game my grandnephew was playing was anything to go by, then all that will be left by now is a few hardy souls desperately fighting for survival and powerups. The game had been remarkably coy on the prospects for a geriatric with a heart murmur.

The hallway lights blink off and then back on again, and I quicken my tottering pace with one single-minded and all-consuming aim—a cup of tea before the power and gas goes out, forever. A last post-apocalyptic cuppa. And I'm close now, real close.

I should have known Ms Prenderghast would be waiting for me in the kitchen. Or rather the ex-Ms Prenderghast, the recently departed but not-gone-very-far and certainly not-gone-far-enough Ms Prenderghast. Ms Prenderghast, undead. She's not alone, either, and as Mr Robbins rears up I deal him a swift clout to the ear, and his glazed over eyes roll back and into his head as his top of the range hearing aid takes a direct hit. Even I cringe at the piercing whine that spills from the shattered device. Thick black blood runs out of his other ear and he wobbles and then drops untidily to lie on the recently mopped linoleum floor.

Ms Prenderghast will not be so easy to defeat. She's not an eighty-year-old man in a bowtie and with a thin wisp of hair carefully combed over his shiny pink pate. Ms Prenderghast is a pitbull of a woman with matronly hips and a fearsome chest, her sleeves rolled up to show her muscular arms, her sensible shoes dangling below prodigious ankles, and with a lifetime of suppressed rage suddenly cut loose.

She snarls, baring her bloodied teeth, and I experience an epiphany as she lumbers towards me. Silvia, Muriel, the decapitated Jeannie, even Mr Robbins—this isn't a zombie plague spread like wildfire by the infected. I have no idea whether or not my fellow denizens of the home have the inclination, but what I am damned sure of is that most of us simply don't have the teeth for it. No, this is a one woman crusade, a zombie Typhoid Mary, the simmering fury born of years trapped in a job she hates, of looking after the incontinent, the infirm, the senile, erupting like a dynamited dam into a mind swept clear of all other thoughts. Ms Prenderghast is a malevolent force of nature, a berserker, and here am I, stood directly in her murderous path.

I'm kind of surprised my heart doesn't give up then and there. Perhaps it's the sight of the hot water urn gently steaming away behind her. Perhaps it's just that I already know how this is going to play out, so what's the point of getting overly excited about it?

Only, as the calm descends and as I take a half step back to press against the tiled wall, something red catches my eye. It's the defibrillator unit, ripped open, and with the charge light blinking green.

I grab the paddles, and Ms Prenderghast does the rest. Really, I don't move after that. I'm not sure I could have if I'd wanted to. She stumbles forward, trips over poor Mr Robbins, and her bullet-shaped head connects with a sharp zap as I'm still trying to read the upside-down sign on the paddles that warns: "FOR USE ON THE CHEST ONLY."

I'm not certain she's dead. I mean, deader; no longer *un*dead. So when the green light flashes once again I stoop and carefully hold the paddles against the greying hair at her temples, hold them until the unit is discharged, until there's a faint and unpleasant smell of burning. Even so I'd do it again, just to make sure, but my knees can't take any more. I'm too exhausted and, like the defibrillator, spent.

I totter over to the urn, bypass it and with shaking hands reach for the backup kettle. This cup of tea demands properly boiling water. I'm even going to warm the cup up first. It's just a shame it's not bone china, that delicately thin pottery that elevates a mug of tea into something *epic*.

I'm just taking my first tentative sip when there's a soft exhalation from behind me and I turn to see a once-again vertical Mr Robbins looking at me with undisguised hunger. At the door, a couple more mashed up faces lurk, Muriel, and Silvia, and even Mrs Woods, her denture-less gums dribbling bloody saliva down her wrinkled chin. Liver-spotted hands reach across the threshold, a chorus of bronchial moans fill the air. I know what drives them on, and I suspect I'm the last person alive in Berrylands who can give them what their turned-to-mush brains ache for.

I slowly put my cup down and as clearly and as loudly as I can, I say "I'll make a pot then, shall I?"

Liam Hogan is an award winning London based writer. His short story "Ana" appeared in Best of British Science Fiction 2016 (NewCon Press) and "The Dance of a Thousand Cuts" appeared in Best of British Fantasy, 2018. More at http://happyendingnotguaranteed.blogspot.co.uk or tweet @LiamJHogan

THE FINAL BITE

Laurie Axinn Gienapp

(From the diary of Harry S.)
I NEVER PLANNED THIS, I never expected it to happen. I was happy as a human, a twenty-four year old attorney in a prestigious law firm. Not married, but I had my designs on a lovely young woman.

It's rather ironic; we attended a party just three nights ago, and one of the many topics of conversation was vampires. Half of the group feared them, the other half didn't believe they existed. I fell into the latter camp.

And now… now… I've become one of them.

I feel like my life is over. Which it is, of course. Except that I continue to exist, and apparently shall do so, forever. But my life—I mean my existence— has totally changed.

I have so many things to learn. On the one hand, I can go outside during the day, which is a pleasant surprise. Better yet, I don't have to wear sunscreen. For some reason, vampires don't burn. On the other hand, I've had to learn the art of applying color to my face, because we also don't tan, and our ultra pale complexions make us stand out like a sore thumb.

◆◆◆

A Mentor and a Friend

"Hello, I'm Harry."

"Good to meet you, Harry, I'm Clarence."

We shake hands and settle ourselves in a booth in the corner. Clarence appears to be just a few years older than me, but of course I know better than many that looks can be deceiving.

The waitress comes over and Clarence orders two glasses of red wine. We sit there in silence, waiting for her return, and then departure, before we turn to the matter at hand. There is no need to rush, as we both have literally all the time in the world. Clarence appears calm and comfortable; I am anything but. Finally, we have our libations in front of us, and privacy.

"Harry. The Council has asked me to speak with you."

He pauses and I remain silent, not knowing what to say.

"Actually," he continues, "they've asked me to mentor you. It's very unusual to lose one's—shall we say, maker—especially so soon after becoming a vampire. I'm sure you have many questions, and I'm here to answer them for you."

"Why you?"

Clarence laughs. "Not a question I'd anticipated, but one that I can certainly answer. I've got nearly a century of experience as a vampire, so I know the ropes, as they say. But you and I look close enough in age that no one will question our friendship." He pauses. "And frankly, while I don't mind being your mentor, Harry, I truly do want to be your friend."

◆◆◆

(From the diary of Harry S.)
Clarence and I have relocated again. When one does not age, one cannot spend more than a decade or so in the same place.

I can't believe I'm saying this—I, who once was certain that vampires were merely a myth—but I'm truly enjoying my life as a vampire. Clarence has persuaded me that I don't need to keep saying existence instead of life. "It's just a different type of life, Harry," he keeps saying. And I've decided he's right.

◆◆◆

A New Era
"Harry! Over here!"
I'm not sure who said that, the club is so noisy tonight, but I head over to the large rowdy group where I'm welcomed with many pats on the back. Someone puts a glass of warm blood in my hands.
"A toast," I say. "To the new era."
"To the new era," the others repeat, and we all

19

drink heartily.

"I can't believe you did it," one of the women says.

"You mean *we* did it."

Clarence steps up to me and puts his arm around my shoulder. "Doesn't really matter who did it, what matters is that humans finally understand that we don't want to kill them, and we don't even want them for our minions, we want to peacefully coexist."

"Hear, hear!" someone shouts. And once again, we all raise our glasses and drink deeply.

◆◆◆

(From the diary of Harry S.)

Today I celebrated twenty years in the same place. Now that all of humanity believes in us, and believes—no, comprehends—that it would be foolish for us to hurt them, it's no longer necessary to run or hide.

Life is truly good.

◆◆◆

(From the diary of Harry S.)

An odd thing happened today. Clarence and I were taking a stroll in the park, and we saw a young couple walking with their daughter in a stroller. She had golden hair that almost glowed, and Clarence was quite taken with her. As he gazed at the child, she dropped her toy. He picked it up and dusted it off. When he reached out to hand it to her, the child bit him. The parents were quite apologetic and we just brushed it off. Clarence made a joke that the little girl was paying him back for all the years when vampires bit humans, and we all laughed. But I have a bad feeling about this. I mentioned this to Clarence, and he teased me about my premonitions that never amount to anything. I know he's right, I have no reason for this feeling, but still....

◆◆◆

(From the diary of Harry S.)

I can't believe what's happened. It's unheard of, literally unheard of.

Hematologists from all over the world are running all sorts of tests, and scrambling for answers. But the answers are all wrong. The experts are saying that Clarence is no longer a vampire, he's back to being a human. A mortal human. Worse yet, he's got some sort of bizarre anemia. I feel like this is some sort of a sick punch line to a bad joke.

◆◆◆

(From the diary of Harry S.)

I visited Clarence today. He doesn't look mortal, he's as pale as he always was. But there is something about his skin tone, or texture, or something. You can tell he's not well.

On my way over, I stopped at the local blood bank and picked up a couple pints—I remembered that his favorite was O positive. I didn't know he couldn't drink blood anymore. It broke my heart to see him gazing at the bottle, wistfully.

(From the diary of Harry S.)

The media is having a real heyday with this. "Give the gift of life; bite a vampire." Some of the headlines are a little different, but they all carry that same message. After all the time Clarence spent training me to think of my vampire existence as life, we're back to having a mere existence. While some humans seem sympathetic to our plight, this is becoming a real problem. Whether it's being done as a game, or a challenge, or some other reason, more and more vampires are being bitten by humans.

To our knowledge, Clarence was the first to be bitten, or at least the first to develop the sickness. Sadly, he's got a lot of company these days.

(From the diary of Harry S.)

After all the testing, scientists have finally determined that two separate things happen when a human bites a vampire. It isn't just that the bite turns the vampire human. The bite also transmits something called Humanum Viral Anemia. While it's not clear when the Humanum virus first came to be, apparently it is present in—and non-harmful to—all humans. And it's not deadly to vampires, or rather former vampires. It just leaves the former vampire weak, prone to illness, and in constant need of transfusions. Vitamins don't help, and eating foods typically thought of as "iron-rich" doesn't work. All of this is particularly ironic in light of the fact that the formers (that's what we are now calling former vampires) can no longer take blood "the old fashioned way", but must receive an actual transfusion. Some formers have tried complete exchange transfusions, but that doesn't work either. Within hours of the complete exchange, the virus reappears in the former's blood.

◆◆◆

A Last Visit

"Clarence. How are you?" I ask the question out of courtesy, because it would be apparent to anyone that he's not well. But he plays the game.

"Not bad, Harry, not bad. It's good to see you." He pauses. "It's been a while."

I shrug. "You know how it is."

It's not wise for me to be seen in public these days. We're in a small out-of-the-way bar that Clarence has assured me will be safe.

He sighs and then coughs, putting his handkerchief to his mouth. I'm not certain, but I believe I see a spot on the linen. I inhale softly, and I know it's blood.

Clarence finishes coughing and sits still for a moment, catching his breath.

"I'm dying, Harry."

And I realize it's true.

"Is it the anemia?"

He shakes his head. "No. The transfusions

keep that under control. And as long as I don't think about it too much, I'm okay with a constant diet of chicken."

It's my turn to shake my head. "What an odd disease this has turned out to be." I pause. "So then, why are you dying?"

Clarence laughs, and when he looks me, it feels like he's looking into my soul. "I'm mortal, Harry. My time is coming. Haven't you been following the news?"

"No. For the same reason I haven't seen you in awhile. I've been hiding."

Slowly, he nods. "Of course. Forgive me. Well let me bring you up to speed. The scientists have continued their research on us. Not only have they confirmed that HVA cannot be cured, they've also come up with some fancy formulas with regard to the life expectancy of a former vampire."

"Do you have long?"

"I could have a few more years if I wished. But I guess I'm tired of living, Harry. I had twenty-nine years as a mortal, followed by a few centuries as a vampire, and it's now been over a decade as a former vampire. I'm tired."

He quits talking, but I can tell there's more.

"I've stopped the transfusions, Harry. And I'm refusing the vitamins they're trying to force on me. So, no, it's not long."

To my surprise, I see tears in his eyes.

"But I needed to see you, Harry, and tell you that I truly cherished our friendship."

I'm even more surprised to realize there are tears in my eyes, as well. And to realize that I have no words. But Clarence seems to understand all of this. He stands up, and I join him. We embrace, and with no further words he walks out.

♦♦♦

(From the diary of Harry S.)

Perhaps it was fate, perhaps I just wasn't paying attention. But I've been bitten. It was certain to happen. Once again, the media has taken control of the situation. It became a game among them to track down the last few vampires. Because, indeed, there are only a handful of us left. The news reporters don't bite us of course, they'd much rather have the story. They just use all of their resources to track us down. Then they announce where we are, and stand by with their cameras at the ready. What ghouls.

♦♦♦

(From the diary of Harry S.)

After that final conversation with Clarence, I decided it was important to keep up with the news. I'm not sure if that was the right decision or not; I've read things I'd rather not know. But I've made my decision. I know the consequences of being bitten, and I'm not willing to drag this out. I'm not going to a doctor, I am not going to get transfusions.

♦♦♦

(From the diary of Harry S.)

If the media is to be believed—and I think they are this time—I am the last. They are calling me the last vampire, but of course that's wrong. The last vampire has been gone for years. I am the last former vampire.

I've been good at hiding, and I've been lucky. They know I'm out here, but they don't know where.

I think back to how humans once feared vampire bites—which was ridiculous. Our bites granted immortality. It is the bite from a human that is the fatal one.

I can feel my systems shutting down. It's nearly over, and I'm not sorry.

I was going to destroy this diary. After all, I wrote it for an audience of one. But as I've been re-reading portions, I've decided to leave it here, to be found with my remains. Perhaps there are some lessons to be learned from all of this.

Laurie Gienapp lives in northeastern Massachusetts with her husband and their two cats. She and her husband spend as much time as they can either ocean fishing or ballroom dancing. The cats spend as much time as they can, sleeping. Her sci-fi/adventure story "The Weatherman" was published in 2016, and she has had a number of short stories appear in Read on the Run anthologies, since then. Irregularly, Laurie posts to her blog at www.teapotmusings.blogspot.com.

AT WIT'S END

Catherine Valenti

STEPH PLOPPED IN THE overstuffed chair, briefly wondering if she'd have the strength to get out of it. What an exhausting day and a fantastic finish to the opening week of SJ Java, the eclectic coffee shop she and Jonas had opened. They had prepared for a slow start but the steady stream of customers through the door exceeded both their expectations.

They'd had at least one mini-crisis per day. Running out of creamer, a glitch with the espresso machine, and apparently clumsy, although very apologetic, customers who knocked mugs and saucers off the tables. Still, it had been an adventure, and at the end of each day she was exhausted in a good way.

"Steph?" Jonas paused on his way to the kitchen, clutching an armful of the day's newspapers and napkins.

She glanced at him and leaned forward in the chair.

"Don't get up," he said. "You deserve a break here. If I didn't have to get home to feed the cat I'd pull up a seat and join you. I just wanted to let you know I've finished gathering trash, and washed down the coffee machines."

"We were both hopping all day." Steph gave him a smile. "You and I make a great team."

"Hey, it was fun, although a bit crazy. Good thing we had Jenny coming in for the morning rush, but we might need another person to help if this is going to be the norm."

"I guess that's a good problem to have." Steph sighed and leaned back in the chair. "Just dump the papers in the recycle bin and go home. You've done more than enough for the day."

"Okay, partner." Jonas grinned at her. "I'll be back tomorrow, mid-morning. You sure you don't want me to help you open at o-dark-thirty?"

Steph laughed and waved him off. "Go, I'll be fine. I might just spend the night in this chair. I'm pretty comfortable right now!"

"I'll get the lights," Jonas said as he walked to the back door. She was lucky to have him. Not sure how those stars had aligned but if Steph could clone him she would.

The overhead lights went off, leaving only the kitchen light on and the table lamps glowing. She heard the door close and the lock click.

Jonas was an old friend from high school. They'd kept in touch through college, when she took business classes and he focused on all computer science. Even though he had his own computer tech business, he'd jumped at the chance to partner with her to open a coffee shop. "Steph," he'd said, "I love coffee, and I'm certain I would love to work with you." He'd told Steph he needed to be around people, since building websites and working on databases all day—and whatever other techie things he did—left him alone too much of the time.

Yes, he was definitely a godsend.

Steph shifted in the chair, and thought briefly about getting up, but a sudden wave of exhaustion overcame her. There were still a few last-minute chores to finish to get ready for the morning, but for now Steph let her mind drift off—until someone brushed against her right shoulder, sending cold tingles up and down her arm.

Her eyes popped open and she leaned forward, scanning the room full of lamp-lit shadows. No one was there, she was alone. Her heart pounded as she put her hand up to her shoulder. It wasn't only the touch, but the sense that someone had been with her, and it felt so real. Slowly her chills dissipated.

"Silly," she said aloud, jumping a bit at the sound of her own voice. "I must have drifted off to sleep, that's all." The front door was locked, she had made sure of that as the last customer left. Jonas had gone through the back, and she'd heard the click as he locked up. She was over-tired, that was all.

Steph pushed herself out of the chair. Although her feet hurt from standing and walking all day, she needed to prep for tomorrow.

29

Even with all the customers they'd had this week, there were plenty of supplies for the next few days. No need to go to the store tonight for last minute cream or sweetener. The sanitizer had finished its cycle and Steph used a clean towel to wipe the last bit of dampness off the utensils, coffee cups, and plates and arranged them on the shelf. She pulled a box from the lower cabinet to restock the paper items, and a sudden cold wisp of wind whirled around her shoulders. Once again tingles shimmied down her back.

Was there an open window somewhere? The shop wasn't that big, and she was certain Jonas hadn't opened anything. Still, it wouldn't hurt to take another look.

The kitchen window was secured, and she moved through the main seating area, checking that the front windows were locked. For good measure Steph went to the rooms off the main area and checked the latches on those windows. She straightened a few chairs in the second room, and took a good look around.

The house had been vacant for many years after its owner had died and it had fallen into disrepair. The sole heir, a woman who lived overseas, finally got around to putting it up for sale, and Steph and Jonas bought it for a great price, making it a bargain even with the extensive renovations that were needed. It had been built in the early 1900s, and all of the renovations had been done true to the era.

It was Jonas' idea to convert these former bedrooms into private areas that could also be reserved for meetings. The rooms were spacious enough for three tables each, and several small bookshelves lined the walls. She and Jonas had picked out wallpaper and white wainscoting that seemed to fit the personality of the home, and agreed it had improved the ambience.

Jonas had also suggested adding used books to their coffee shop for customers to read as they tested out their drinks from the menu, and Steph agreed it would be a great idea. She and Jonas had scoured estate sales and thrift shops, buying a couple dozen titles.

They did much of the labor themselves to save money, and were in the process of renovating the storage room off the kitchen when Jonas found the door hidden behind floor-length cabinets spanning the back wall. The door had opened to a steep, narrow set of stairs going up to an attic. She had no idea this house had such a room, and apparently neither did the former owner or the realtor, because it hadn't been mentioned in the house description.

The attic had been finished in dark wood wall paneling matching its hardwood floor. A few worn throw rugs covered part of it. The room was long and narrow, and dull light filtered through a tiny narrow window covered in grime. Thick branches from the oak tree in the back of the house brushed against the outside of the window.

The only items in the room were a dust-covered antique writing desk and a heavy wooden chair. A simple wood box sat on a corner of the desk.

Steph had slid off the metal latch that secured

the lid of the box and slowly opened it to uncover a tall stack of yellowing paper, loosely bound with thin twine. The top page had three lines of neatly handwritten script and appeared to be a title page.

At Wit's End
by Julius Victor Harrington
June 23, 1911

A quick scan of more of the stack showed pages covered in identical handwriting. They pulled out three more similar bundles.

"Someone's manuscripts, I think," Steph had said, delighted at such a find. "I wonder if these have ever been published."

Jonas flipped the yellowed pages of one bundle. "These are amazing. We definitely need to find time to go through them. I bet there's a great story here, and not just on the written pages."

They'd taken the box downstairs, and decided to keep the manuscripts in the shop's safe until they had time to go through the papers. Every few days Steph thought about taking a look at the stories but the shop renovations and opening week kept her and Jonas physically and mentally exhausted, and she wanted to wait until she had some time to relax and give them a good read.

It hadn't happened yet.

A flicker from the headlights of a passing car startled Steph out of her reverie, and she found herself standing in front of the desk they'd brought down from the attic. A gentle breeze encircled her, and Steph heard a whisper in her ear. She jumped, and again chills traveled up and down her back.

"C'mon Steph," she said aloud, and shook off

her discomfort. "This is ridiculous." No one was here. No one had touched her shoulder, or whispered in her ear, and there was no breeze. It was just jitters from a week of exhaustion. Nothing a good night's sleep couldn't cure.

◆◆◆

Steph unlocked the front door forty-five minutes before the scheduled six o'clock opening. A restful sleep had done the trick, and she was ready for the day. She heated water for tea and prepped the coffee machines. As soon as they were ready, she poured her first cup of the day, and since she had a bit of time, checked the inventory list.

Fifteen minutes before opening she heard a knock on the door and saw the delivery van parked out front. Fresh pastries from Carol's Creations, and right on time. Steph opened the door and Carol walked in, carefully balancing a tray of scones and sweet rolls.

Steph breathed in the yeasty cinnamon aroma, and sighed. "Carol, what a divine smell!"

Carol set the tray on the counter. "That's the idea."

"I might need to up the order since we sold out early yesterday."

"Okay, just let me know." Carol picked up her tray from yesterday, and paused. She looked around the room, then her gaze came back to Steph. "Everything good here?" She paused. "You know, with openin' week and all."

"It was busier than I thought possible. And so

33

nice meeting all the customers."

"Nothin' strange?"

"Well..." Steph stopped herself. How would she explain the odd happenings from last night? "What do you mean, strange?"

Carol took a few steps toward the door. "Oh, I don't know." She paused and half-turned toward Steph. "There are stories, that's all."

Steph furrowed her brows. Before she could form a response, Carol was already walking out the front door.

"Uh... thanks and see you tomorrow," Steph called out. Carol didn't turn around but waved a hand.

Steph closed the door, shaking her head. That woman had crazy baking talent, but she was an odd duck for sure. Never said more than a few words at a time but she managed some curious conversation today. What was that bit about "stories" anyway? Was she suggesting ghosts, maybe?

"As if I really believed in them," she told herself. Steph was logical. Ghosts were not logical. There were plenty of explanations for the breeze, and whispers, and even the sense that someone was touching her. Lack of sleep, the air conditioning coming on, sounds from the ice maker. She pushed the nonsense away. There was work to be done.

Steph spent the next few minutes arranging the pastries in the glass case, and making a quick sweep through the shop for any last-minute cleaning. Satisfied that all was in order, Steph turned the closed sign to open, flipped the lights on, and unlocked the door a few minutes before six.

It didn't take long before the first of a small rush of coffee lovers came through the door. SJ Java was in a perfect location, convenient for commuters to stop in on their way to work, and great for foot traffic for locals in the neighborhood. Steph managed to handle them all without much delay.

Jonas sailed in through the back door at eight.

"Your timing is perfect. The crowd just left." Steph grinned and took a step away from the register. "Time for my break so it's all yours, barista!"

Jonas laughed and gave her an exaggerated bow. "I've got this, just let me wash up first."

A loud crash and the tinkle of glass breaking came from the seating area. Steph and Jonas sprang into action. Jonas headed for the closet to get the broom and Steph grabbed a handful of dish towels and a trash bag.

"I'm so sorry," said the young woman standing over the broken mug and plate. "I didn't think it was so close to the edge and I must have bumped it by accident."

"Please don't worry, accidents happen," Steph said as she bent down and carefully picked up the larger pieces of stoneware. The black and white checked floor tile looked beautiful in here, but anything breakable that hit it didn't stand a chance. Maybe they'd polished these table tops a bit too well, they'd lost quite a few mugs and saucers this week and even the flatware had gone flying. "Stay where you are, I don't want you stepping on any of this."

Jonas came out with the broom and dustpan and swept the mess off the floor while Steph mopped at the spilled coffee with one of the towels. "What drink did you have?" she asked.

The poor woman had such a concerned expression, she appeared near tears. "I... uh... I... Oh, I'm very sorry."

Jonas glanced up at the woman, who was now wringing her hands. "No harm done, as long as you're okay." He looked at Steph. "She had a caramel macchiato."

"Got it." Steph carefully folded up the towel to keep the broken glass in, then smiled reassuringly at the woman. "I'll be right back."

By the time Steph had returned to the table with a freshly-made drink, Jonas was using a clean towel to wipe the table and take one more swipe on the floor. Steph placed the steaming mug on the table. Right in the middle.

A late morning lull gave Steph and Jonas time to regroup in the storage room while Jenny watched the counter. It didn't take both of them to inventory, but it offered them a chance to meet and plan for the next week.

"Jonas, does something seem... weird to you around here?"

He finished his check-off of cups and napkins for their next order, then glanced at Steph. "Other than a computer geek owning half a coffee shop?" He gave her his cute lopsided grin.

"You're a nut!" Steph put her checklist on the shelf. "Seriously, while this past week has been fun and crazy busy, it's also been really strange."

"In what way?"

"For starters, all the broken mugs and plates, and other things that seem to be flying off the tables and counters."

Jonas laughed. "I wouldn't say any of them actually flew." He crinkled his brow. "I do agree we have had what seems like more than our share of breakage, but it is the first week and we have to expect a bit of chaos. Don't we? Maybe everything will stabilize when we get into a groove."

"Maybe," Steph shook her head. "It doesn't seem to be a stabilizing thing. It's happening to random customers as well as the two of us and Jenny. I just find it odd. And then what Carol said..."

"What did Carol say?" Jonas had turned his attention back to the items on the shelves.

"She asked how our first week was going, and if anything odd was happening."

Jonas shook his head. "Besides the fact that she's an odd duck herself?"

"Hey," Steph said, smacking him lightly on his arm. "Not nice. She just doesn't talk much. But it does make me wonder why she would she ask something like that out of the blue?"

Jonas turned to Steph. "You got me. Maybe the place is haunted, and whoever is here isn't a coffee aficionado." He grinned.

Steph frowned. "After what happened last night after you left, that's not very funny."

The smile left his face. "Wait, you didn't mention anything. What happened?"

Steph sighed. "It's really not that big a deal, but putting it together after the week we've had with so many broken mugs... we either have a poltergeist or the customers and the three of us are the clumsiest humans I know." Steph shook her head, and felt the same chills from yesterday. How crazy would Jonas think she was? He dealt in techie-stuff where everything was black and white and could be logically explained.

Her legs were suddenly a bit wobbly and she sat down on the stool. Jonas pulled up a wood crate, took her hands in his, and stared intently into her eyes. "Are you all right?"

"After you left, I think I might have dozed off in the chair," she said. "It felt like someone touched me and woke me up."

"Wait, someone broke in?"

"No, no one was here. I checked everything, even the doors and windows."

As she gave him a recap of her encounter, she grew more certain it really could have been a ghost, or spirit, or something paranormal. It wasn't only the feeling she had of being touched, but the unexplainable sense that she was not alone and someone was trying to communicate.

Steph couldn't interpret Jonas' reaction. He raised his eyebrows a few times, shook his head a bit, and finally his gaze went up to the ceiling.

After what seemed like an eternity, Jonas stood, pulling her up as well.

"Say something, Jonas," Steph said,

wondering how delusional he thought she was.

"I think," he said, "we need to do some checking on the history of this house."

◆◆◆

Steph and Jonas worked out a plan, and early that afternoon Steph was on her way to the county courthouse in search of land records. She hoped the county kept old property information on site.

She made her way to the property records area, and asked for help from the middle-aged woman behind the desk. "You're in luck," the clerk said. "We have records way back to the late 1800s. The new ones are online and you can access them here on the public computers, but the older histories are available on microfiche."

"That's great news." Steph had half-expected to be told she'd have to wait for the information, but the clerk led her to the back room thick with huge metal file cabinets.

"We check the computer first for the address, then it should give us the file location of the property history." Steph sat in front of the computer and typed in the shop address. A long list of names popped up.

The clerk turned and looked at Steph. "Hey, that's the address of the new coffee shop that just opened at the old Muldoon place," she said. "I grew up in that neighborhood. Are you the owner?"

"Yes, one of them," Steph said. "Do you know the place?"

The clerk shook her head. "Don't know a lot

about it, but I've been in this town since I was a kid, and that place has had more owners than any other around here. They just don't stay. Some people claim it's haunted."

"Do *you* think it's haunted?"

"Oh heavens, no!" The woman laughed, shaking her head. "I personally don't believe in spirits, but I do believe that old houses have too many creaks and groans for some folks."

Steph nodded half-heartedly, but the thought of the strange goings-on made her wonder. She scanned through the document on the screen. "How can I find out who lived in the home in 1911?"

It didn't take long for the clerk to find the right file cabinet and pull the microfiche. She showed Steph how to use the reader, and left her on her own.

Just after five o'clock Steph stepped out of the courthouse with a couple pages of notes. She stopped by her favorite Chinese restaurant for takeout, then to the store for a six-pack of beer, and hurried back to SJ Java.

By the time she arrived Jonas had just closed up and was wiping down tables. He glanced up and smiled at her. "I managed to get most of the customers out of here early, and just have a few dishes to take care of. I had a little free time before Jenny left and I managed to do some internet searching while you were gone. It took some digging but there's some interesting information on Mr. Julius Victor Harrington."

She set the food on the counter. "I have some information too. Let's finish up here and we can talk."

Between the two of them, they made short work of cleaning up, and were soon settled in, serving up food from the take out cartons. Jonas set Harrington's box of manuscripts on the side of the table.

"Tell me first what you found," Jonas said between bites.

"Interesting history of this house." Steph took a drink of her beer. "We knew when we bought it that it was built in 1905. Harrington was the original owner.

"So that confirms Harrington did live here," Jonas said, scooping up another spoonful of rice.

"Right. Then in December of 1912 the house sold. There were well over a dozen owners after that. The clerk at the courthouse told me for the last thirty years none of the owners held the property for very long, and many of them rented it out. Apparently the clerk lived down the street from here until about five years ago, and had noticed lots of moving in and out by renters. It sat empty for a year after the last owner, the woman we bought it from, moved overseas."

She took another look at her notes. "That's all I have. Your turn," Steph said. "What did you find out?"

"Harrington was the editor of the local newspaper, and quite a bigwig in town. His wife had died in 1906 in childbirth along with their baby, and he never remarried." Jonas took one last bite, and Steph waited impatiently for him to finish chewing.

41

"Apparently he was also a writer, although not published, which of course explains the manuscripts in the attic. Harrington was involved in a legal battle in early 1912. He'd accused one of his employees, a copy editor named Robert Waldron, of stealing his latest manuscript and publishing Harrington's story as his own."

"Was it one of the manuscripts we found?"

"I don't think so." Jonas opened the box and pulled out the yellowed pages. "I looked through all four titles, although it's possible Waldron changed the name from the original. I couldn't dig up a copy of the book that was published. But that's not the interesting part."

Steph pushed her plate aside. "Don't keep me in suspense."

"The story was a big success, and that's when Harrington realized it was his own stolen work. Harrington hired the town's best attorney and brought a lawsuit against Waldron, who of course swore up and down he'd written every word. Waldron even had the manuscript in his own handwriting, but Harrington maintained he'd copied it word for word from the story Harrington himself wrote, then accused Waldron of destroying the original. Everyone in town had an opinion, and there were more than a few fistfights over the whole thing."

"How did the legal battle turn out?"

"It didn't. The day after the trial started Julius Harrington was found hanged from a tree outside his home." Jonas took a deep breath. "This house."

Steph's eyes widened. "He killed himself?"

"That was the official story," Jonas said. "The judge dismissed the case, and I guess Waldron won out by default. But Harrington's friends maintained to their dying days he'd been killed, and probably by Waldron, although they couldn't prove it."

"How horrible." Steph shook her head. "Poor Harrington. I feel sorry for him. That is, if he really did write that book."

A sudden gust of wind tore by the two of them, and plates and cartons went flying off the table. Steph screamed, and Jonas managed to snag one of the beer bottles before it tumbled to the floor.

The box and the manuscripts remained safely on the table.

"What the..." Jonas jumped up and looked around the room, then back at Steph, who was holding on to the edge of the table. "Are you okay?"

"I think so," Steph said, her voice trembling. She slid out of her chair and stepped closer to Jonas. They surveyed the mess on the floor.

Steph picked up the top manuscript, "At Wit's End", and waved it around. "I guess Julius Harrington wants us to know he really is the author of the published manuscript."

Steph was putting the finishing touches on the Halloween decorations scattered around SJ Java. Tomorrow was going to be even busier than usual as they'd planned on staying open a little later and passing out candy to the trick-or-treaters.

She finished arranging the ceramic ghosts and

witches on the table tops, happy that it had been a long time since they'd had to worry about tumbling tableware. She looked up as Jonas burst through the door, carrying a large box.

"Are they here already?" Steph asked. She guided him to a clear spot on the counter where he set the box down.

Ever since Julius Harrington had made his feelings apparent, Steph and Jonas had worked to get his four manuscripts digitized, edited, and published. When "At Wit's End" became a bestseller, they started in on the others since they had an audience eager to read more.

This was the final published story by Julius Victor Harrington. "Trouble in Threes" was as humorous as the first three, and if it was anywhere near as popular she expected the copies they'd just received would fly off the shelf.

The publicity was great for business, and the past few months had been crazy busy. She and Jonas had hired three more baristas to handle the crowds.

Jonas pulled out a book, then passed it to Steph. She flipped through the pages, then closed it and sighed. "This is my favorite cover."

"You say that about all of them!" He leaned over and gave her a little kiss. She smiled and kissed him back.

It had all worked out wonderfully. Their business and the relationship they hadn't even been looking for had both blossomed.

"I am a little sad," Steph said as Jonas thumbed through his own copy of the book.

He nodded. "I feel the same way. This is it. The last one."

"Not just that." Steph wadded up the tape from the box and tossed it in the trash can. "I'm also sad that we weren't able to track down that stolen manuscript—we haven't been able to find a copy of it anywhere."

"I know," Jonas said. He gave Steph that lopsided grin she loved so much. "But we're not giving up on it. There's got to be a copy stashed away somewhere, in someone's attic, or a used bookstore, or a library."

Steph nodded. "You're right, we will find it. We'll figure out a way to republish it, with Julius Victor Harrington as the rightful author."

A soft swirl of air brushed past both of them.

"You're welcome, Harrington," they said in unison.

By day, Cathy is a mild-mannered reporter for a national online news service for lawyers and news media. After hours, she is an editor, runs a small publishing company with her business partner, and writes paranormal and science fiction stories as well as motivational non-fiction.

She has a short story in "The Ancient," an anthology by a group of authors known as the Seven, as well as stories in several of the Read on the Run anthologies, and is currently working on a novel.

Cathy lives in Idaho, where in addition to writing,

she enjoys hiking, running, skiing, and dancing. Visit her website at https://catherinevalenti.com

A GOOD BOY

Desmond Warzel

STITSKY SAT ON THE edge of the bed, forking mouthfuls of take-out rigatoni from a Styrofoam container. *Star Trek* had just ended and now the battered old television emitted the singular strains of the *Sanford and Son* theme. Stitsky didn't care for the show, but the remote control was bolted to the nightstand, out of his reach, and he was much more interested in his dinner than in changing the channel anyway.

The kid sat slumped in the room's only chair, which had been pushed against the far wall. In one hand he held a plastic fork, with which he poked at a second container of rigatoni balanced on the arm of the chair. The other hand was shackled to the old-fashioned radiator below the window.

Stitsky hadn't intended to handcuff the kid at all, but the little sneak had already ditched him twice that day. At twelve years old, even with his sheltered upbringing, the kid was already slipperier than any fugitive or bail-jumper Stitsky had ever dealt with.

"Eat up there, partner. Gotta keep that energy up. Big day tomorrow." The boy looked suspiciously at the pasta which oozed globules of white cheese, and the side order of bread, soaked through with butter. "No dice? Man, you woulda been better off growing up in my neighborhood. This is *real* food. I think you're missing out, living in that penthouse."

"Damn right I am." These were the first words out of the kid's mouth in hours, and swearing clearly didn't come naturally to him; even this mildest of profanities had not come without a slight but audible hesitation. To strengthen his tentative outburst, he shoved the take-out container off the arm of the chair. The pasta left red tracks on the threadbare carpet, and the bread sailed out and landed face down.

Under ordinary circumstances a tantrum like this would have been worth a grounding; in some households, perhaps a paddling. These circumstances were far from ordinary, however, and Stitsky was not reined in by parental instinct. The kid had been sawing away at his already-frayed nerves all day, and this last tiny cut threatened to sever the whole works. Before the last of the spilled rigatoni had rolled to a halt, Stitsky was off the bed and yanking the kid as far out of the chair as his cuffed wrist would allow. He retrieved a small but deadly-looking gun from inside his jacket and waved the barrel in the boy's face.

"If you're a big enough pain in the ass, I'll let you go, right?" he hissed. "Let me correct your thinking. This *Ransom of Red Chief* stuff doesn't fly with me. You piss me off any further, I'll just shoot you, stuff you in a storm drain, and tell your parents you got away from me. I got three justifiable homicides on my record. I'm not bragging, just letting you know I'm capable of pulling this trigger. Understand?" The kid nodded, drawing back against the window. Outside was only blackness.

"Good." Satisfied with the scare he'd imparted to his young charge, Stitsky shoved the boy back into the armchair, and knelt to clean up the mess. "I don't know what you think is so great about the streets. There's nothing out there for you. The cops pick you up, they'll just call your parents. Anybody else picks you up, well, I'll leave that to your imagination." He stood up, stretching his aching back, and tossed the container into the wastebasket. When he turned around, the kid was watching him. He seemed thoughtful; Stitsky hoped the little punk was weighing what he'd just said, and deciding not to push his luck any further.

But he *wasn't* a punk, that was the thing. Stitsky's gut told him that this was a good boy, or at least a boy who *tried* to be good. This attitude he'd been copping, it was a front. The kid was in over his head, scared half to death, and he was *twelve*, for Christ's sake.

Stitsky sat down on the bed once more and resumed his meal. He tried, unsuccessfully, to feign interest in Redd Foxx's antics on the television, and when he glanced over at the armchair, the boy was

49

rubbing absently at his wrist, the beginnings of tears shimmering in his eyes.

Aw, hell.

"All right, ace," sighed Stitsky, reaching for the tattered phone book atop the television. "What do you want on a pizza?"

"Cheese."

"Just cheese?"

"Yeah."

"You're a real sensualist, you know that?"

The pizza arrived thirty minutes later and Stitsky ducked out into the hallway to pay, not wanting the delivery guy to see the kid shackled to the radiator and get any ideas in his head. He gave the guy a ten-dollar tip; he'd just expense it to the boy's parents.

The delivery guy wasn't five minutes gone and the boy had the pie three-quarters eaten. Stitsky finished his rigatoni—now practically cold as ice, but still delicious—and watched TV. Now it was *Green Acres*.

The kid polished off the last slice of pizza in two bites and wiped his mouth on his forearm.

"What's *Ransom of Red Chief*?"

This was the first conversation the boy had initiated since Stitsky had caught up with him that morning.

"How's that, kid?"

"You said you didn't want any *Ransom of Red Chief* stuff."

"It's a story. By O. Henry. Outlaws kidnap a kid and hold him for ransom. The parents don't pay, because they know the kid's such a brat the crooks'll let him go. Which they do. Don't they make you guys read in school anymore?"

"I don't know. My parents homeschool me."

"Somehow I'm not surprised." Stitsky rose and collected the empty pizza box and the other trash and dumped them in the wastebasket. He kicked off his shoes and fell onto the bed, sprawling across the faded comforter. He reached for the remote and idly flipped through the channels. "What do you wanna run away for anyway, kid?"

"I don't know what you mean."

"You got both parents, still married, who obviously care about your well-being. They're sparing no expense to get you back; trust me on this, young man, because I'll be able to retire on what I'm gonna make off of you. You got a beautiful home. I've been in it. You got video game systems in your room I never even heard of."

"So?"

"So what am I missing? Running off, that's pretty desperate. Especially for you, because let me tell you something about yourself, you weren't meant to be a child of the streets. You don't have it in you. You'd stick out like a sore thumb out there."

The boy hesitated for a long moment, and then blurted out, "They hit me."

"No, they don't."

The kid's eyes widened. "Huh?"

"If anything, they're overprotective of you. Kid, give it up. You can't lie worth a damn, and you

51

shouldn't try anyway."

"You don't believe me?"

"I strip you down, I guarantee the only marks on you are the ones I put there today."

"Um... well, they haven't done it in a while."

Stitsky sighed. "Kid, I deal with the worst people on the planet—"

"No, you only think you do."

"I liked you better when you were quiet."

"Yeah, join the club."

"Look, you're a good boy. I can tell. I know people, sometimes better than they know themselves. I have to. Everyone I run down, they got a sob story, and usually I couldn't give two shits. But you... well, there's a missing piece to this puzzle, and I'd love to know what it is."

Nothing.

"Suit yourself." He got up and turned the lights off, set the alarm on his mobile phone, and flopped back down on the bed, still dressed. The TV, which Stitsky's interrupted channel-surfing had left on CNN, now provided the only illumination in the room. "Try and sleep, we're getting an early start tomorrow."

A few minutes later, the boy spoke up again. His voice seemed very small in the darkness. "They never let me go out."

"That's a little more like it. Go on."

"I study at home. I'm not allowed to have any friends. When I get sick, the doctor comes to see me. If my parents have to go somewhere together, someone watches me to make sure I don't leave."

"That's pretty tough, man."

"You know the first thing I did when I got away from them?"

"What's that?"

"Went to the movies. I'd never been."

"No shit? *Never*? What did you see?"

"Everything they were showing."

Stitsky couldn't help laughing. He looked over toward the window. The boy's face shone like the moon in the light from the TV, but his eyes were lost in shadow. "There's more," the kid said solemnly. "But I don't think you'll believe me."

"That's up to me, isn't it?"

"I guess you like stories, right? Like the one you said before, by the candy bar guy?"

"O. Henry. Right."

"Because this is a weird story."

"Go ahead."

"My parents know this guy—they've known him since before I was born. He's—like a priest, I guess, or a minister, but I don't think he has a church. He doesn't have a cross, or one of those star things. He always comes to the house. His name is William—I don't know his last name. My parents do whatever he says. My father says listening to William is the reason he got so rich and successful. So he does whatever William tells him to. I think my parents give him money sometimes, too.

"Once every month, William comes to the house, and he brings these other people with him, and we go into the room. We have this room my parents keep locked up, and inside it's black everywhere, and crazy stuff written all over the floor and the walls. And candles everywhere. And

William and his friends put on these black things, like judges wear, and light the candles, and sing these creepy songs. My parents sing, too. They all drink wine. Sometimes they bring something in a cage, like a cat or a rabbit.

"They kill whatever's in the cage. With this big silver knife. The animal is usually quiet when they bring it in, but it always screeches real loud when they hurt it.

"I have to stand in a big circle in the middle of the floor.

"William says he can feel me getting stronger every time they do it. He says I'm different from other people. He says I'll be able to do stuff I can't even imagine. He says I can make everyone do what I want... "

The boy's voice trailed off. He stared straight ahead, avoiding eye contact. Stitsky lay quietly, considering the boy's words. He finally turned over on his side, facing toward the door, and tried, with limited success, to repress his laughter.

"What?"

"Never seen a movie, huh? You gotta be kidding me. I might've been born on a Monday, but it wasn't *last* Monday."

"Oh."

"You're one in a million, kid. I take back what I said before. You sure can spin a yarn."

"I had to try."

"Aren't you gonna try to convince me? I think a story like that warrants a little commitment on your part, don't you?"

"Forget it."

◆◆◆

Stitsky had always been a light sleeper, and over the course of his career he had necessarily honed this skill to a keen edge; he could depend on himself to come alert at the slightest disturbance and to do so reflexively. It was this skill which now served him faithfully; he sat immediately upright, without a conscious thought, and came face to face with the boy, sidling between the foot of the bed and the TV stand. He had presumably brushed against the comforter on his way by and inadvertently triggered Stitsky's awakening. The boy made no sound but his eyes filled with panic. The handcuffs, now empty, dangled from the radiator. Stitsky launched himself at his errant charge and they crashed to the floor in a tangle.

Stitsky recovered first and hauled the kid to his feet by his shirt collar. "You little prick! I can't believe I felt bad for you!"

"Why can't you just let me go!" shrieked the boy. He struggled against Stitsky's grip, arms and legs flailing in every direction. "I never hurt anybody! I never did anything to anybody!"

"Shut your mouth!" Stitsky had allowed his guard to drop. Even uncooperative, the kid had been a welcome change from the sort of person he was used to dealing with, and this sentiment had left Stitsky vulnerable. Well, no more.

"I try to be good!" the boy screamed, tears flowing freely down his cheeks.

"Try harder!" Stitsky tried to wrestle the boy

onto the bed, but the youth still resisted, and the two of them blundered into the open closet. Half a dozen theft-proof hangers made discordant music above them. When the pair landed, the boy was on top.

"I hate this!" The boy clamped one small hand on Stitsky's wrist, and blinding agony raced all the way up to his shoulder. Stitsky felt like he had thrust his arm into a raging bonfire. Wisps of smoke curled up from his jacket sleeve where the boy gripped it. "Just let me leave! Please!"

Stitsky gritted his teeth and slipped his free hand inside his jacket, fumbling for his gun. The boy redoubled his grip, and the pain engulfed Stitsky's entire left side. When he was finally able to grasp the weapon, the intense heat of the metal raised blisters on his hand as he drew it.

"I just want to be good," whimpered the boy. Stitsky could barely hear the lamentation over the hammering of his own pulse in his head. He tried to hold his shooting hand steady even as the gun itself cooked the flesh of his palm. For the first time in years, the thought of money fled him entirely; his sole concern was his immediate survival. His vision began to dim, but even with the quivering of his ruined hand, even though the only light came from the still-flickering TV, he was able to aim squarely between the boy's eyes. In the brief interval before blackness overtook him, Stitsky saw that those eyes now burned a deep crimson. The gun dropped to the floor. Beneath it, the fibers of the carpet began to smolder.

◆◆◆

Still sobbing, the boy scrambled backward, away from Stitsky's twisted, blackened body. His chest heaved. He held his hands up to his face, staring at them, hatred smoldering in his eyes. He struggled to his feet, trying not to look at the closet. Smoke hung in the air; it burned his eyes and gagged him with every breath.

"I just want to be good," he whispered, and slipped out into the hallway, closing the door silently behind him.

Desmond Warzel is the author of a few dozen short stories; most of these are in the science fiction and fantasy genres, but he takes the occasional delight in subjecting his characters to the uncanny and supernatural. His work has appeared at beloved websites like Abyss & Apex and Tor.com, in ear-pleasing audio on newfangled podcasts like Escape Pod and The Drabblecast, and on genuine dead tree in nifty magazines like Shroud and the venerable Fantasy & Science Fiction. He lives in northwestern Pennsylvania.

THE SPREE

Jessica Lévai

AS THE COUNTDOWN BEGINS, I flex my fingers on the handle of the shopping cart and try to quell my mounting excitement.

Tonight I, the Vampire Countess, Mistress of Night, who have seen empires rise from nothing and sink to dust, so mysterious and aloof I have rarely left my castle in over a century, find myself under the bleaching fluorescents of the local Stop-Mart, waiting to begin a three-minute shopping spree. That I won. In a raffle.

Not a single word of that makes any sense. Yet here I am. How did this happen?

My familiar retrieves my mail every day from the post office, and rarely do I see it before she has sorted out and destroyed what is of no use to me. But she was derelict, once, and I found a complete stack. I was too delighted by the novelty to chide her. I spent hours in my drawing room, fascinated

58

by the slick papers that promised low-interest credit and discounts on cars, a glimpse of a world beyond mine.

But it was the invitation to the raffle that grabbed me. I read it over and over, large print and fine. It should have meant nothing. My fortune is secure. Food practically throws itself at me. But as I stared at the shelves of my library full of books I had already read, I found that centuries of being the monster, draining men dry, surviving as a ghost in my own home, had finally worn thin. I sneaked out of the castle myself to put my entry to post.

"Why would you do such a thing?" my familiar had asked. She held the notification of my winning in her hand and was perfectly furious, which only amused me. I gave her no answer. I owed her none, but the truth is, I wasn't sure what a suitable answer would be. And that uncertainty, which should have been uncomfortable, was so unlike my usual experience that I found it delicious.

"Ten! Nine! Eight! Seven!"

I shake these thoughts from my head and attempt, in these last seconds, to strategize. I must appear human, push the cart at human speeds. I must buy the sort of things that humans buy. I have some idea what those are.

The crowd of people at the starting line continues their countdown. "Six! Five! Four!"

I retrain my focus. I shall buy what I need.

"Three! Two!"

I shall buy what I want.

"One!"

But I have no idea what that is.

"Go!"

The cart clatters as I give it a starting push, cornering with surprising ease through a blizzard of confetti. I skip the bread and frozen food and head for Health and Beauty, thinking of the sort of things my servants bring back from their trips to the market.

I make my first selection and deposit three bottles of mouthwash in my cart. It's essential for one with my diet, if one wishes to avoid smelling like an abattoir. True, there was one gentleman I entertained who told me the mouthwash reminded him of his alcoholic cousin, but I didn't give him much time to regret the comment. I roll next to shampoo and conditioner, because these tresses do not stay voluminous and tangle-free on their own. I pick up a little foundation while I'm at it, and replenish my supply of purple eye shadow. No, I've never really thought it was necessary. But there are some things that are expected.

Now I'm in the laundry aisle, and I spend precious seconds locating that particular detergent that takes care of my darks *and* works in my high efficiency washing machine. Two jugs of that and a couple gallons of bleach, and suddenly I'm glad that they aren't going to be weighing my purchases. There's an awful lot of liquid in this cart, even if the grocery store doesn't carry the liquid I need. At the end of the aisle there are scented candles and I help myself to four of them. They make the castle much more livable. And I do have rather a soft spot for lavender.

It occurs to me that I can't see the countdown

clock from this end of the store. Mentally I figure that I've been at this for about fifty-two seconds. I decide to skip the next aisle; I never drink wine.

What next? Pasta and beans. That's funny. It's been a whole minute now; I need to focus. Everything I've taken so far is useful. But I am not satisfied.

I head over to the meat counter. There are some really tempting steaks. (Please don't; I've heard it before.) I ask the worker behind the counter to ring up five of them for me. They're good and bloody and even if I can't get everything I need from them, they will come in handy if I have guests. I smile at the idea. I should throw a party. While the steaks are being wrapped, I take a quick look at the produce section. Absolutely nothing I need here. I could pick up garlic, but I don't have time to waste on irony.

The crowd at the finish line continues to roar. They're eager, and I am, too. Ninety seconds or so, half-done.

My familiar and I spent a week preparing for this spree, planning my outfit and practicing mannerisms so that I could pull this off with no one suspecting anything. As I slipped into the role of normal human woman and embraced it, I realized I wanted to feel like one, if only for a little while. So here I am, running an errand, groceries in my cart, a regular car waiting for me in the lot. It's happened, and yet, there's something missing.

I must head home, soon. And I must feed. There are stores in my castle which will sustain me for tonight, but soon I will need to hunt someone, seduce him, and destroy him. For all my pretending to be human, this must be. I remember my last meal, his tenderness, his gentle smile. If I were human, perhaps I could have loved him, and he me. But that is impossible.

Pensive and distracted, I've been dawdling. Thirty seconds remain. If I am not back out to the car in reasonable time, my familiar will come in after me, with weapons if necessary. I sigh out loud as I head back to the starting line. Dreams simply cannot be realized at nine p.m. on a Saturday night at Stop Mart.

But perhaps they may be indulged.

I turn the cart with more force than is wise and head back to the middle of the store. Soon the people at the front are going to start chanting again, counting down. There will probably be more confetti.

Here we are. The books. They are in the same aisle as baby food and diapers. I didn't use to think that made any sense, but now I understand. There are humans looking for the same thing I am. Change. Adventure. To be carried away by love or at the very least, romance without dangerous consequences.

There are so many covers. So many beautiful men, so many fluttering damsels. Some of these damsels are tough, and at least one of them seems to be a monster slayer. That won't do. But there are those who glow in the man's presence, reflecting his strength as he towers over them. I wonder what it feels like, to receive that kind of attention. I think I knew once, but it was long ago.

I pick seven of the most attractive covers and toss them into my cart. There's just enough time to wheel my way to the finish line before a harsh buzzer goes off through the public address system.

I am congratulated as pairs of hands emerge to help me fit my winnings into the reusable bags I am given as a bonus. Since I am one of the few shoppers who might actually last longer than this non-woven propylene will in a landfill, I decide to accept graciously. I am offered an escort to my car as another courtesy, which I decline politely. Someone is taking pictures and I play along, though I'm sure the photographer will be dismayed when none of them quite turn out. By the time they come to ask me to take more, I will be long gone.

Out in the parking lot, my familiar loads the car's miniscule trunk with my haul while I slide into the back seat, one of the books in my hand.

I'll never be able to come back to this store. Well, not for a few years at least. But that worry is a small one, and so very far behind me, as we start the drive home. The only thing that I see before me now is an evening to myself. I shall pour myself something to drink, and curl up with a good book.

Jessica Lévai has loved stories and storytellers her whole life. She studied history and mathematics in college and went on to earn her PhD in Egyptology. After eight years of doing the adjunct shuffle she devoted herself to writing full-

time, and you can read her work online at Luna Station Quarterly and Body Parts Magazine. Links to these and more can be found at her website, JessicaLevai.com. She currently seeks a publisher for her first novella, a vampire romance in Pushkin sonnets. She has begun work on her second long-form piece and dreams of one day collaborating on a graphic novel, and meeting Stephen Colbert.

RUN FOR THE ROSES

Gerri Leen

Zombie Horses can't be beat, doo-dah, doo-dah, Just be careful what they eat, oh, doo-dah day.
21st Century Folk Song

"THEY JUST GOT SO FRAGILE, those old-time race horses. One, two, maybe three races and boom, a condylar fracture, or a sesamoid break. Out for months, maybe for good. Retired to stud, to breed more of the same. It's why we don't use them anymore." Ramon carefully patted Zero Tolerance on the neck as the reporter watched. The horse bared his teeth and eyed the hand that fed him, with something very different than affection. "You just do not want to fall off these horses."

"I saw the footage from Gulfstream Park."

"Maybe they shouldn't have called that filly Man Eater?" Ramon laughed. "These babies will

65

run for days if you have the right bait."

Squalling infants would have been the best lure, but the public would never have gone for that. Instead, thrillseekers signed up to ride the pace truck. They skipped bathing for three days so the "still alive" smell was ever so clear to the horses— horses that were run with muzzles but no whips. Whips were useless on them, didn't make them go—no pain, no gain. But brains... oh yeah, these horses would run all day and into the night for some brains.

Fresh, though. Cadavers were of no appeal. Dummies rubbed with raw meat didn't fool them, either. Horses weren't the brightest of animals, but they were bright enough.

"Ramon, what do you have to say to the public outcry that racing should be stopped?"

"Because one jockey got eaten?"

"With a lot of people watching, between the simulcast and ESPN coverage."

Ramon shrugged. "Real Thoroughbreds can't cut it. And people don't like to watch Quarter Horses the way they do Thoroughbreds. Personally, I'd rather watch a mule race but they make these babies look like pushovers when it comes to being trainable." He patted Zero Tolerance on the cheek and nearly lost his fingers when the horse lunged at him.

The reporter was studying the horse. "Why do you work with him?"

"Why do lion tamers do what they do? Why do fighter pilots?" He laughed. "It's fun."

"It's idiotic. That horse would eat you in a

minute if he got loose."

"Yep, he sure would." Ramon sighed. "Lady, you have no idea what it was like before the zombie horses. I was a rider before I became a trainer. I was nearly killed when Cyber Warfare broke his leg in the stretch of the Belmont. There's never been a zombie horse broke down that way. Never."

"I accept that. But the old-time horses didn't eat people. Did you hear that this morning at Zia Park, a zombie horse veered off the track during morning works and ran into the group of clockers."

"Seriously?"

She nodded. "He bit three of them."

"Yikes." He shook his head. "They're off to Zombie Nirvana, then. Damn shame. People willing to rise in the dark just to clock horses are few and far between."

"Your empathy is touching."

"The owners don't pay me for empathy. They pay me to get their horses to the finish line first."

"And you're the most successful trainer to do that. I mean look at Zero Tolerance—the favorite for today's race, right?"

Ramon tried not to preen.

"What's your secret?"

He smiled. "Creative feeding."

She took a step back.

"Not humans. You think I could get away with that in this day and age? Everyone is tracked." He smiled. "But there are other warm blooded creatures."

"I don't want to know." She seemed to shudder. "You realize I'm going to use this in the

67

story."

He shrugged.

"You want me to use it, don't you?"

He laughed. "If other jockeys think my horse here has recent experience with live meat, they may get a little spooked on the track. And this race is big. We both know that."

She nodded. "The biggest." She turned to the cameraman. "We've got what we need. Go get this filed."

The cameraman packed up and left in a hurry, probably real happy to get clear of Zero Tolerance.

"You're not going to edit it?"

"Why bother? You orchestrated this from the beginning to say exactly what you want." She moved closer to Zero Tolerance. "I don't think you feed him live meat."

"No?" He touched her hair. "I could feed you to him."

"You could. If you want to spend the rest of your life in prison." She turned to look at him. "Or Zombie Nirvana if they decide to make the punishment fit the crime."

He dropped his hand. "Just joking around."

"I'm not." She smiled in a way that was distinctly creepy, then moved to the stall door, closing it—closing them in with Zero Tolerance.

"What are you doing?"

"The job I was hired to do."

He waited for Zero Tolerance to try to nip her, but the horse was ignoring her. "What the...?"

"*Eau de Corpse*. We all know zombie horses won't touch a corpse. It's what David Marsh uses when he works with Captivate."

"Marsh?" Marsh had gone on record saying he was going to win today, that Captivate would take the race by a huge margin.

"He may have paid me to do this." Again the creepy smile. "There'll be an inquiry. The horse will be quarantined until the issue is resolved. The race"—she reached over and unhooked Zero Tolerance's tie-down—"will be long over by the time this boy races again. Do you think his owners will send him to Marsh once you're dead?"

The horse sniffed her briefly, then turned to Ramon, blocking his way to the exit.

"Why?"

"I get five percent of the winnings. That's not chump change. Also—just like you said. It's... fun." She laughed softly as she leaned against the wall and crossed her arms across her chest. "Bon appetit, horse."

Zero Tolerance's big white blaze was the last thing Ramon saw before the pain began.

Gerri Leen lives in Northern Virginia and originally hails from Seattle. In addition to being an avid reader, she's passionate about horse racing, tea, whisky, ASMR vids, and creating weird tacos. She has work appearing in Nature, Escape Pod, Daily Science Fiction, Cast of Wonders, and others. She's edited several anthologies for independent presses, is finishing some longer projects, and is a member of SFWA

and HWA. See more at http://www.gerrileen.com or tweet @GerriLeen.

SMITTEN

Ginny Swart

CUPID SAT ON HIS USUAL perch just above the mirror of the bus, watching the passengers board.

He was looking out for two regulars who, he'd decided, both looked as if they'd be just right for Michael. Sally, with her short pleated skirt and bright curls bobbing up and down and her wide smile for everyone. And Grace, more serious, with straight brown hair and a sweet, rather withdrawn air about her.

Perhaps he should aim his dart at Sally. Michael himself was quiet and shy and from long experience, Cupid knew that opposites attract.

Sally climbed on board in front of Grace, had a laughing word with the bus driver and then started down the aisle to the back of the bus.

Right, Sally it was. Cupid fitted a tiny silver arrow into his bow and let it fly. Immediately Sally rubbed her neck irritably. The job was done.

Cupid was determined that this morning they'd start a meaningful conversation.

Three mornings of "Cold today, isn't it?" from Michael and three replies of "Too right!" from Sally was enough of an ice breaker for most people but this time, he knew things would move forward.

A stout middle-aged woman made for the empty seat next to Michael but just at the last minute, she hesitated for no reason and moved further down the bus, leaving the place free for Sally. Haven't lost my touch, thought Cupid complacently, flitting to the edge of the window above the two of them.

Come on now, boy, you go first.

Michael Harrison's briefcase slipped from his lap with a *thunk* and as he bent to retrieve it, he touched Sally's leg.

"Sorry," he mumbled.

"No worries," she said. "That bag looks pretty heavy. What do you carry in it? Bricks?"

"Nope. Books," he smiled. "Computer instruction manuals, mostly. I'm a travelling Mr Fixit for badly behaved computers."

"Wow. You must be so *clever.*" Sally blinked her enormous blue eyes which had an immediate effect on every man she looked at. "I've only just worked out how to post pictures on Facebook."

"So you don't use a computer for work? I thought just about everyone did these days."

"Not me. I work for a caterer. I spend my days cooking fancy food for other people's dinner parties."

"You sound like a real old-fashioned girl."

Michael smiled then blushed. "In the nicest possible way, I mean. Cooking's good."

"Oh, do you think so?" Sally giggled. "The funny thing is, after five o'clock I don't go near a stove. I just live on take-away, Chinese mostly. That's my favourite."

"That's odd, I love to cook. Well, bake actually. I make all my own bread—whole wheat, rye, ciabatta, you name it."

"I've never met a man who made his own bread. Isn't it difficult?"

"No, it's really easy. Oh sorry, here's my stop. Nice talking to you, um—?"

"Sally Abbott," she said, taking his hand.

"Michael Harrison."

Sally watched Michael as he alighted from the bus and twinkled her fingers at him as he looked back, just as Cupid had known he would do.

Yesss! He exulted.

He looked across at Grace, who was also watching Michael as he walked off. Cupid recognized the look, a mixture of longing and admiration. Sorry, Grace, he said to himself, Sally got on the bus first today, so she's the one.

The following day he had to keep three people from sitting next to Michael before Sally made her appearance, flushed from running for the bus. Cupid was exhausted with the mental effort of guiding unwilling passengers to seats they hadn't aimed for, but relaxed once Sally was safely sitting next to Michael.

"Hi," she said. "Phew, nearly didn't make it. I overslept as usual."

"Hello Sally." His huge smile of welcome warmed Cupid's heart. The boy was well and truly smitten. "I hoped I'd see you this morning. Here, I made this for you."

He produced a small seed loaf, still warm from the oven.

"For me, really? That's so cool! Ta!" Sally held it up and inhaled dreamily. "This smells divine. I'll have some as soon as I get to work. While it's still warm."

Good lad, thought Cupid. Bread's better than flowers, it shows serious intentions.

"Ten dollars says it'll never happen."

Cupid looked up, annoyed.

Somehow his skinny, miserable alter-ego Eros, with his cynical outlook on life, had wormed his way onto the bus and was hunkered down on the seat behind Sally. "This one's far too sharp and sassy for that slowpoke. He hasn't even asked for her phone number yet."

"Ten dollars? You're on," snapped Cupid. "Anyway, what do you know? These two are perfect for each other. Now hoof it, this bus is my beat. Get back to your Picadilly circus across the sea."

"Tch! Just paying a friendly visit." Eros stood up and flew slowly out of the window. "Remember to keep me posted so I can collect my cash."

Cupid scowled. He hated the thought that he was in any way connected to this self-satisfied misery. It was ridiculous the way being immortalised in bronze had turned his head. Nevertheless, Eros had managed to shoot a faint dart of worry into his mind.

What did he really know about Sally, besides the fact she was bubbly and cute and Michael had fancied her since the day he saw her a month before?

Michael on the other hand, he could vouch for. He'd been riding to work on this bus for three years and shown himself to be an upright citizen, kind to old ladies, hard working, and polite. And he made his own bread.

From what Cupid overheard the rest of the week, things between his two protégés were going excellently and although they hadn't actually dated yet, there was talk of seeing a film together on Friday.

But on Friday Michael missed the bus. He'd been waiting for the crust of his rye loaf to reach just the right shade of perfection, and this had taken ten minutes longer than he'd expected.

So after looking around and seeing that Michael wasn't there, Sally sat alone and opened a book. She was still reading when a good-looking young man stopped next to her.

"This seat taken, baby?" he asked cheekily.

"Ronnie!" she shrieked. "Fancy seeing you here! No, of course it's not taken… sit, you lovely man. So, how's life with you?"

Cupid scowled.

Yadda yadda yadda. My goodness, this girl could talk! All about a rave-up at a club that lasted all night, and bombing around the town on the back of a bike belonging to someone called Boris, and how she'd got herself a fabulous tattoo and if

Ronnie was a really good boy, maybe he'd get to see it one day.

Cupid started to have deeply second thoughts about Sally.

And then she said, "What, tonight? With the whole gang? Love to. I've got a vague date with some nerd but that's easily cancelled."

Cupid thought *that's it!* You double-crossing little minx! You are *not* the one after all.

♦♦♦

On Monday Michael made his way to his usual seat and at Sally's stop he watched the door hopefully, but she didn't get on. How could she, the poor girl had broken one of her high heels and had to limp back home for another pair of shoes.

Cupid, who made the bus with only seconds to spare himself, after nearly wrenching his back while he heaved up the paving slab, smelled the delicious ciabatta loaf in the paper bag and could sense Michael's disappointment. Poor lad.

Grace was sitting across the aisle from Michael and the smell of the ciabatta made her lift her head and sniff appreciatively.

"Warm bread!" she said softly. "That reminds me of my father's bakery."

"Your dad was a baker?"

"Yes. We lived above the shop and I woke up every day to the wonderful smell of bread baking below."

"That must have been nice."

Michael looked at her for the first time. She

76

had a low musical voice and a curtain of shining brown hair framing a sweet face, innocent of any make-up. Cupid could tell he was thinking that she was just how a girl should look. "So, did you learn to bake too?"

"Of course! Dad had us all down in the bakery making the specials—you know, focaccia, rye, seed loaves... that's a ciabatta you have inside there, isn't it? I can smell the olive oil."

"You're right. And I've added some whole olives too. I thought I might try it with dried tomato next time."

"That could be good."

They smiled at each other, one baker to another.

Cupid felt a pang of guilt at his own stupidity. How could he not have seen that Grace was perfect for Michael? But what luck he'd realised in time.

Now all he had to do was keep Sally from getting on the bus and charming Michael all over again. Young men were so vulnerable to the wiles of girls like her.

The following day, Sally failed to appear. Some stinging nettles had inexplicably made their way into a bunch of flowers she'd been given by the lovely Ronnie, and she'd come out in a painful rash. The day after, Cupid excelled himself and jammed the elevator in her block of flats so the poor girl was stuck for two hours, calling and shouting.

He'd judged it just right. Three days was enough to do it and when Sally finally boarded the bus, Grace and Michael were sitting close, their heads together over a book Grace had brought to show him. *Breads of the Mediterranean*. Michael didn't even notice Sally.

Cupid sat above them, satisfied with a job well done. Even if he had to admit to a false start. He just hoped Eros wouldn't fly in and crow over his lapse of judgement.

But moments later he was aware of a malevolent little snigger. His wretched alter ego was back again.

"So, what did I tell you?" Eros fluttered up and plonked himself on the ledge, smiling nastily. "A disaster. I knew it would be, she wasn't his type at all. Come on, cough up."

Cupid found a ten dollar note rolled up in his quiver and passed it over.

"One little mistake every hundred years or so isn't a train smash," he said loftily. "And at least I've corrected my error in time. Unlike some I could name."

"What are you hinting at, you fat, pathetic excuse for a matchmaker?"

"I could mention names such as Brad and Jennifer. Nicole and Tom. Madonna and Guy. And other fiascos in higher places that the Official Secrets Act forbids me to talk about. But I've too much class to rub your nose in your failures."

Ginny is a South African who lives in Cape Town, and is the short-story tutor for three on-line writing colleges in South Africa, England and New Zealand.

Her preferred occupation is writing short stories, and she has over 700 accepted by magazines and anthologies all over the English speaking world. She has a couple of forgettable romance books out there too. She is still hoping to write The Big Novel but until then, shorts will do just fine! Website: https://ginnyswart.com/

THE LAY OF THE LAND

Jude-Marie Green

MR. SMITH HOWLED AGAIN like to bring down the moon.

"Shush, old dog," Jannie said. She rattled her keys. She'd been given them a few hours ago when she'd accepted the job. Keys for the fat padlocks on the gates, keys for a guard shack, keys for a place to live, an old trailer planted next to the abandoned park. They'd hired her fast and the pay was more than the going rate, and the hiring manager didn't even question Jannie using her own dog on patrol. Which was good, because she'd never patrol without him.

Jannie and Mr. Smith paused before a sagging arch with a ruined sign. Lake Town Amusement Park, in big letters. A few dim safety lights glowed. Nothing stirred.

She stepped forward. Mr. Smith sat down.

"Whatcha doing, dog?" She tugged on his

leash. The Rottweiler stood up slowly and sniffed at the air. She waited for him to make up his mind. Mr. Smith sniffed at the air and slowly walked through the gate one stiff leg at a time.

"Good dog." She scratched behind his ears.

He gazed up at her with mournful eyes. He listened to her with more attention than anyone she'd ever known, including gentlemen-friends, which was a good thing, since they were all gone and she still liked to talk.

She locked the gate behind them.

"Time to patrol," she said. Mr. Smith's ears perked up. "Let's check out the Ferris wheel, on the other side of the park. We can work our way back from there and get the lay of the land."

Mr. Smith whuffed in agreement.

Her flashlight, a rechargeable rubberized monstrosity that didn't need a carry-license the way a baton did, provided enough illumination to avoid the hazards of a path crazed with dry clods and weeds that grew in colorless tangles. Mr. Smith walked close to her legs.

"You'd think there would be lots of little critters," she said. "Rabbits or squirrels or rats or something." The weeds stayed motionless under the huge moon. No lambent eyes peered at them from ground level.

Her flash glinted on a door-sized metal rectangle on the ground. She kicked some dirt loose from it, revealing a sign. "Take A Spin On The Ferris Wheel!" The ghosts of bright paint shined through the rust flowers. Jannie pulled it free from the weeds and leaned it against a white rail. She

81

traced the words with her finger.

"That, Mr. Smith, is a work of art," she said.

The Rottie didn't sniff at the sign.

Jannie aimed her flashlight at the Ferris wheel's seats. Wood and chain rusted quietly under the slight illumination.

"What a relic," she said. "Wait a minute. Is that someone up there?"

Her flash sketched a human-shaped shadow in a seat about halfway up.

"Hello!" she shouted. "What are you doing up there? You need to come down right now!"

The shadow did not move. The Ferris wheel groaned and shook and rotated a slow inch upward, taking the shadow closer to the top of the ride.

Jannie ran to the control box at the foot of the ride. The box sagged open, its mechanical guts spread out and entwined with ivy and Queen Anne's lace.

"No way," she breathed. The wheel inched around its circle. She stood on the platform as empty seats spun by. When he got here, she'd make him show her how he got the ruined Ferris wheel to turn. Then she'd detain him and have the cops haul him away. No way was she going to let a trespasser go, not on her first night, not doing something as all-out dangerous as this.

The turning cogs squealed like tortured souls. The chair she awaited slid onto the platform. All the noise stopped at the same moment. The Ferris wheel went as still as if it hadn't been moving at all. No one was in the chair.

She stared into it, checked the corners and the

outside of the seat. No one could have climbed out, not while she was watching. She'd seen the shadow just a moment before the seat arrived. Her attention hadn't shifted. Still, the chair was empty.

Something touched her leg. She screamed and staggered away from the touch.

Mr. Smith looked at her with apologetic eyes, his tailed tucked between his legs. He nuzzled her leg again.

"Yeah, yeah," she said. Her heartbeat slowed to its normal pace. "I don't suppose it was some random... an accident... maybe I didn't see anything after all." She took a ragged breath, let it out, then took a deep breath. She felt steadier now.

"I don't believe in ghosts, Mr. Smith. You shouldn't, either. Why, we've patrolled warehouses and parking garages and cemeteries and the worst we've seen is vagrants and horny kids. But I wonder if that ride was rigged to spook people. Yeah! That's all. They saw us coming, Mr. Smith."

The dog licked his chops.

"C'mon, Mr. Smith, there's a lot more of this park to patrol."

She turned her back on the Ferris wheel. Chills skittered up her spine but she clenched her teeth until they stopped. She couldn't let the situation spook her.

"And if that was a ghost, so what? What's that to us, Mr. Smith?"

She took hold of Mr. Smith's leash and strode away, certain she'd hear the rusty squeal again, but all she heard was silence.

Mr. Smith guided her on a safe path around the

83

lake. She swung the flashlight in a steady arc. Still water gleamed under the moonlight. The water smelled fresh enough. A wooden dock stretched into the lake.

She stopped by the broken signboard at the entrance. Her flash illuminated a faded notice.

"Stocked with catfish during the season," she read. "Sure looks empty now. Couple months from now, we can have ourselves a hush puppy fish fry, what do you say to that?"

The dog grinned.

"Looks safe to me, Mr. Smith. Let's check it out."

They walked onto the gray boards of the dock. It shimmied under them and waves slapped against the wood. Boards creaked under her boots.

"Not safe enough. I don't think we need to patrol all the way out there."

Mr. Smith turned with her. The boards screamed and broke. His claws scrabbled on the wood which opened up, swallowing him. Jannie heard a yip and a thud. Then nothing.

"Mr. Smith!" She threw herself full-length on the dock, staring down into the dark hole. "Mr. Smith!" She shined the flashlight into the hole. Nothing. "I'm coming!"

She swung her legs into the hole and grabbed the edges. "I'm coming, Mr. Smith!"

Before she dropped in after him, she heard the dimmed sound of claws scrabbling. And panting.

"Mr. Smith!" The dog's head appeared, his paws grabbing the shattered ends of the boards. She reached for him. Before she could grab him, he leapt onto the dock, his muscles bunching. He stood splay-legged and panting.

Jannie threw her arms around him. He smelled like mud and stale water, not much like dog. She ran her hands over his chest and back, his belly and legs. "Mr. Smith! You're okay! You got through that without a single injury. Wow, you lucky dog."

She stood up. "Guess we'll need to report this hole, huh, Mr. Smith? Let's get back onto solid ground, okay?" She led him off the dock then turned around. The night was as quiet as ever.

She skimmed her light across the lake surface. Nothing danced on the water. None of the usual lakeside creatures stirred, no birds startled awake or fish jumping for insects.

"What do you think, Mr. Smith?" She frowned. "With all the noise we're making, we should be scaring up flocks of grasshoppers. This has got to be the quietest park I've ever been in. Where are the crickets? The cicadas aren't singing and I don't see any lightning bugs at all. This is the South, isn't it?"

Mr. Smith remained silent.

"Oh hell. I wonder if this is one of those places where they dumped defoliants and bug killers. Agent Orange, like that. Maybe I should ask for hazard pay. And get you some dog boots."

Mr. Smith put his head under her hand and she scratched his ears.

"Awful big place to be so empty. Except for us, Mr. Smith."

The moon rode the sky as she approached the swing ride, a decrepit circle of weeds climbing rotten support posts and tangling in the wooden seats. She wanted to rush by the structure, half-certain that it would mysteriously start moving.

"But it's my job, Mr. Smith," she said. "I'm here to make sure no one trespasses, no one is here who shouldn't be, and no one gets hurt." She swept the ride with her flashlight. "And I don't know about you, Mr. Smith, but I do not see that little girl in the pink dress."

The dog stared at the little girl. Small whimpers escaped him. Jannie wondered if he could smell the bright red blood that caked half the girl's face. She could not.

The little girl's mouth was open wide, her eyes round and shocked. Jannie thought maybe she was screaming without making a sound.

"Oh hell," she said, and ran towards the little girl. "Don't worry, I'll help."

Jannie dropped to her knees in front of the little girl and held out her arms.

"I can help you," she said. "What's your name, sweetie?"

The blood disappeared from the girl's face. Her pink dress changed, the rips mended and dirt cleaned away. Jannie blinked. The little girl was gone.

"Mr. Smith, that was a ghost," Jannie said, her voice hitching like she'd run a marathon and needed a pull on an oxygen canister. The dog held his tail still. She wiped cold sweat from her face and swatted dirt from her uniform knees. "Pardon my French, but what the hell *is* this place? What have I gotten us into here, Mr. Smith?" She patted his head. "Maybe we should pack up our bags and get out of town."

The dog stared up at her. Jannie saw disappointment there.

"Yeah, you're right. Just ghosts. Nothing to get worked up about. Not like they can hurt us."

The dog lowered his head. For the first time that night he strained forward on the leash.

The park was too quiet, but she could hear, ever so distant, early morning trucks on the highway, wind in the grass, some kind of night bird. The Ferris wheel across the park was motionless and the swing chairs did not move.

"I could get used to this, old dog," she said. "Quiet nights, picturesque ghosts. They don't bother me any. Do they bother you?"

Mr. Smith wagged his stubby tail slowly.

Together they walked to the picnic area under a stand of fragrant cedar trees.

Before Jannie could sit down, Mr. Smith growled. Jannie's nerves twanged tense and she stood up straight.

Grass stirred. The slight noise in the utter stillness brought the little hairs on her arms to attention. She swept the flashlight up and across, a slashing beam meant to reveal any threat.

Mr. Smith sprayed a volley of barks.

A young boy and a younger girl, wearing homespun clothes from a bygone era, threw themselves at her, their thin arms circling her waist.

She reached out to hug them. Her arms looked to be full of two children but she could as well have been hugging air.

"Mr. Smith! Here!" Jannie commanded. The

dog came alert, rumbling deep in his throat like a motorcycle engine.

She drew her gun.

"Stop! Whoever's out there, stop now!" She set her feet firmly apart, steady on the ground. Now the children stood in front of her, in front of Mr. Smith, facing the madman.

He was barely taller than the children. Jannie wondered if he was cold, if ghosts could be cold, barefoot half-naked ghosts. He held a knife that gleamed wickedly in the moonlight.

The children shrieked. Jannie's eardrums shook, tinnitus vibrating through her brain. She reached out to touch the children, reassure them. Her hand passed through them.

Jannie's gun hand wavered. What could she do? They were ghosts. She could not protect them from another ghost. Not with bullets.

She slid the gun back into her holster.

The madman ran at the children. Mr. Smith howled and leapt. Man and dog went down in a tangle. They rolled in the grass, silently. Mr. Smith didn't bark and the madman, the ghost, didn't open his mouth. He hit her dog and her dog bit at him. She thought her old dog would win, bring the man to heel or at least run him off. But the madman was stronger. He lifted Mr. Smith in his thin blood streaked arms and hurled him. Mr. Smith slammed into a tree and slumped to the ground, unmoving and silent.

Jannie shrieked.

"No! Mr. Smith!"

She threw herself at the madman. Ghost or not,

he was solid. They grappled. She swung out with the flashlight as she fell but didn't connect with anything. Still, the lens cracked and tinkled, the loudest sound. She fought back, but no matter what hold she tried, she couldn't get a good grip on him.

Finally he had her on her back, his weight holding her down. His hands wrapped around her neck. He grinned as he squeezed. She almost blacked out, close to dying by the hands of a ghost.

Then she heard Mr. Smith howling.

Something smashed into the madman, knocking his hands loose. Jannie could breathe again. She rolled to her knees, coughing. Mr. Smith pinned the madman and had his jaws at the ghost's throat. Jannie heard a terrible snap. The madman sagged. And then he faded into nothing.

With ragged cheers echoing, the children disappeared.

Mr. Smith bounded to her side, a dopey dog smile on his face. He licked her, his tongue rough and wet.

"Oh, Mr. Smith," she crooned, "you good, good dog. Thank you. You saved my life!"

He waited patiently while she struggled to her feet. "No lasting damage, I think, but you saved me just in time. You're a hero, Mr. Smith!" She reached to scratch his ears.

He took her hand in his mouth, gently, and tugged.

She looked at him, frowning. "Okay, dog, show me."

He led her back the way they'd come, across the field and to the lake. To the dock. He didn't lead

89

her to the hole in the wood but underneath, where the pilings met the lake shore. Moonlight shined down, showing a dark lump. He stood over it and waited for her.

She knelt by the lump, his body, and he stood over them both. She pushed aside the broken wood that covered him but couldn't find the injury that had killed him.

"It's okay, Mr. Smith." She reached for him, but her hands passed through the dog's ghost. And he faded away.

She was alone in the park again, with just her dog's body and a busted flashlight.

She stood with her head down. No thoughts in there. No words, either. The eerie silence of the park matched the new quiet inside her. Morning mist rose and dampened her uniform and her face.

She would finish out her shift. Only until six a.m., she told herself. Nowhere else to go. No one to go home to, either.

She struggled to lift Mr. Smith's body, planting her feet and hefting. His ghost reappeared and rubbed against her leg. She bit back her tears, shaking, wishing she could reach down and scratch his ears, but she didn't want to drop his corpse. She draped Mr. Smith across her shoulders, fireman's carry. But where could she take him? Out of here, first off. Perhaps across the valley. She would find a good resting place for her friend in the mountains. Somewhere.

Mr. Smith's ghost walked beside her to the entrance of the park. He did not follow his body outside the gates.

"That's all right, Mr. Smith. I understand." She sank to her knees and wound her fingers in the chain link fence.

"Wait for me, Mr. Smith. My shift is almost done, but I'll come back. These ghosts have settled in. Maybe there's a way we can help them move along, Mr. Smith. Clean up the park and get them, what's that phrase? Lead them into the light. Lead *you*," her voice broke and she whispered the rest, "into the light."

Mr. Smith stayed with her until sunshine dissolved the morning mist. He faded along with it.

She got up from the dirt. She held her cell phone, tossed it up and down in her palm, considering. Finally she pushed a few buttons.

"Yes, ma'am, this is Jannie... yes, the new security guard, I'm just checking in. No, I'm not quitting." She faked a laugh. "No, everything's fine. I guess I'll be staying on." She pulled a hanky from her shirt pocket and absently wiped tears from her cheek. "Yes, ma'am, me and Mr. Smith."

Jude-Marie Green has edited for Abyss&Apex with Wendy Delmater Thies, Noctem Aeternus with Michael Knost, 10Flash Quarterly with K.C. Ball. She has sold short fiction online, to anthologies, and for podcast, recently to The Colored Lens, Toasted Cake with Tina Connolly, and Daily Science Fiction. She won the Speculative Literature Foundation's Older

Writer's Grant and attended Clarion West in 2010. She lives in Southern California. More at her website:judemarie.wordpress.com

DOWN THE ROAD

C. M. Saunders

CAROLINE'S EYES SNAPPED open just in time to witness the brilliant white flash of headlights as the oncoming vehicle veered past within what seemed like inches. With a sharp gasp she steered her little Ford Fiesta back into her own lane. Over the hum of the engine there was an angry blast of a horn. Somebody was telling her off and boy, did she deserve it.

Had she dropped off there for a moment?

Yes, she most certainly had.

Shit. That wasn't good. Especially on this stretch of dual carriageway, which was a notorious accident black spot. She decided to pull over for a few minutes on the hard shoulder and take the short break she had been promising herself for the past twenty or thirty miles.

Slowing the car she checked her rear view mirror. The roads were generally quiet at this late hour and it was dark except for a single set of fading red lights. Her hands were shaking. Damn it, she knew it had been a bad idea to risk driving almost two hundred miles after a double shift at work. But when you get that call, the call that tells you that your father is in the hospital and the end could be near, you don't pause to consider the logistics. You get in your car and drive.

Taking a deep breath she tried to calm her racing heart. Almost there, just one more hour and she could be at his side. Maybe some fresh air would help. She wound down the driver's side window and breathed in a lungful of icy January air.

That was better.

Time to get moving again. Winding the window back up, Caroline slipped the car into gear, released the handbrake and prepared to pull off. That was when there was a sharp tap at the passenger-side window that almost made her jump out of her skin.

"Wha..."

Glancing across she saw the dark figure of a man looming large. A policeman who had taken note of her erratic piece of driving? No, no uniform. Her first reaction was to make sure the doors were locked. They were. God bless central locking.

Drive! Her mind screamed.

But she couldn't move. Her limbs seemed frozen.

The man seemed to take the hesitation as an invitation, and there was a dull click as he tried the handle of the locked door. Unsuccessful, his arm extended and he rapped at the glass again with a white knuckle, this time with more urgency.

Stranger danger!

That was something that had stayed with her since childhood, and even as youth morphed into adulthood and her life became weighted with responsibility, they were still wise words to live by.

But what if the guy was in trouble?

On long journeys she often thought about the story of the Good Samaritan and wondered what she would do if confronted with the same situation. Would she stop to help? Or just turn her head and carry on about her business?

Her mind flashed back to a newspaper article she had read that week. In China, a little girl was struck by a car and lay in the road, alive but badly injured, as traffic and pedestrians passed by without a second glance. The little girl later died, and it was speculated that she might have survived had she been taken to a hospital sooner.

If Caroline drove away and left the man standing in the cold at the side of the road only to later discover something terrible happened to him, it would be her fault and she would never forgive herself. He might just require directions or the use of her phone.

All this passed through her mind in a matter of seconds. And then, as if watching the actions of someone else through her own eyes, she saw her hand reaching for the lock release. There was a smooth *brrr... click!* And the passenger door opened. An icy breeze invaded the car's interior and she shuddered involuntarily.

She thought, hoped, the man would simply

open the door and speak to her. Ask a simple question she could answer in a flash, then she could be on her way safe in the knowledge she had stored some plus points in her karma bank. But without waiting for an invitation, the man slunk into the empty seat and slammed the door shut behind him.

Caroline turned to meet the stranger's gaze. His eyes were deep and dark, hidden beneath brows so thick they almost met in the middle, yet they blazed like twin fires with an intensity she couldn't recall ever seeing in an individual before. They seemed to pull her in, command her attention so much she had to force herself to take in the rest of his face. Almost under duress she noted his pale skin, drawn cheeks, slightly pointed nose and chin and tangled thatch of dark hair. He was wearing a black trench coat, buttoned high to keep out the cold. Not the best outfit for hitch-hiking at night.

"What do you think you are doing?" she asked, willing herself to sound authoritative. She was disappointed when her voice sounded anything but.

"Taking shelter," the stranger replied in a thick, syrupy voice.

She should have been alarmed, but to her surprise Caroline felt no fear. Instead she was filled with the strangest sense of familiarity, almost as if she knew the man. The last time she felt like that was during a chance encounter with a long-lost school friend at an Oasis concert in London a few years previously. How strange. Did she know him? Could she know him? Her mouth opened dumbly as she searched for the right words. "Do you need... directions?" she asked, finally.

"No, I know where I'm going. It's you who needs directions," the stranger in black replied, cryptically. "I'm here to help."

This offended Caroline somewhat. She had been good enough to open her door to this guy, and there he was saying it was *she* who needed help? The nerve of the guy!

Instead of giving him a mouthful, she heard herself say, "Okay... So where are we going?"

"Down the road," came the reply.

Caroline took this as her cue to start driving and, after checking her mirrors, pulled smoothly out into the road. "Car broken down?" she asked, hoping to jump-start a conversation.

"You could say that..."

As they resumed the journey she stole a few glances at her new travelling companion. She couldn't believe she was doing this. Picking up a hitcher? If Dad found out he would kill her, if her passenger didn't kill her first. Oddly, however, she didn't feel the least bit threatened. In fact, she felt quite comfortable in his presence. He exuded calmness and serenity, sitting quietly next to her as they zoomed down the dual carriageway. There was a comfortable stillness between them, and Caroline felt no nervous compulsion to make conversation the way she usually did with strangers. Even more surprisingly, neither did the stranger.

Eventually, however, her curiosity got the better of her. "What do I call you?" she asked.

"You can call me whatever you want. I don't mind," said the man.

"I mean... what's your name?" Caroline

97

pressed.

"Does it matter?" The stranger replied in that deep, throaty voice of his, eyes fixed on the road straight ahead. "Names are interchangeable. What is a name but a means to distinguish one another? And since we are the only two here, I don't see the point."

An unanticipated response, if ever there was one. Why didn't he want to reveal his name? Was he some kind of fugitive? An absconder? Escaped mental patient?

Caroline threw an anxious glance in the direction of the glove compartment where she kept her purse. And her mobile phone. Then it occurred to her that whatever he was, perhaps the man was right. When you thought about it, under most circumstances names were superfluous. Instead of pursuing the matter Caroline shrugged and tried to concentrate on her driving. The road was unnaturally quiet, even for this late hour. She couldn't recall passing a single vehicle since her unscheduled stop.

As much as she tried, she couldn't tear her attention away from the hitcher for long. The man fascinated her. It wasn't sex appeal. She was sure she didn't find him the least bit attractive. There was just something about him, some indefinable quality.

"Where are you headed, exactly?" Caroline asked, wanting to know more about him and finally surrendering to temptation.

"This way," the stranger said, nodding his head at the windscreen.

"How will I know when we reach your

destination?"

"You'll know," he replied.

So he didn't want to talk, preferring to play the role of the enigmatic stranger. Fine. Caroline wriggled in her seat and turned up the car heater. It seemed to be getting colder by the minute. She began to regret stopping to give the stranger a lift, reconciling it with the fact that it had never been part of her plan. The whole thing was an unfortunate misunderstanding.

In the ensuing silence her mind shifted from thoughts of serial killers to more supernatural matters like the phantom hitcher. The urban legend of a lone driver picking somebody up who turns out to be the ghost of an accident victim. At some point during the journey the spectral passenger invariably disappeared. Caroline warily glanced at the stranger out of the corner of her eye, just to check that he was still occupying the passenger seat. He was, and looked real enough to her. So real, in fact, she could see the plumes of vapour issuing from his mouth and nose and hanging in the air as he exhaled. Did ghosts breathe?

Shut up! Caroline commanded herself. She was beginning to freak herself out. The guy was socially awkward, and probably in trouble, but so what? Let's just hope the karma gods were taking note of her selfless actions.

Right now something else was bothering her. She had made this journey umpteen times before, but the particular stretch of road they were now travelling didn't seem at all familiar. Most dual carriageways were featureless. They were designed that way to limit distractions. But there were no road signs, no service stations, no exits. She was sure there should have been one a few miles back. Had she made a wrong turn somewhere?

No, that was impossible. There were no wrong turns to make, unless she strayed off the dual carriageway altogether, and evidently that was not the case. Must be her mind playing yet more tricks on her. Cat's eyes and safety barriers rushed past in a grey blur beneath an empty black sky. No stars, no moon, and still no other traffic on the road.

There was something else. The dashboard clock had stopped, its illuminated hands frozen at 11:27. That had never happened before. She glanced at her wristwatch, only to find that too had stopped, and at the exact same time. 11:27.

Caroline frowned. The whole surreal episode was beginning to make her uncomfortable. "Do you know what the time is?" she asked, unsure of why it suddenly seemed important.

"No. I have never been a slave to time," the stranger replied.

For some reason this bold statement made Caroline chuckle. "As much as we try to deny it, surely we're all slaves to time in our own way, aren't we?"

"Only to a certain point, Caroline. After that... we are all free."

Caroline's breath caught in her throat. How did he know her name? She surely hadn't told him during their sporadic bursts of awkward conversation.

The featureless landscape flashed by outside,

seeming to zoom in and out of focus. Wooziness threatened to overcome her. She blinked and shook her head to clear it. She wanted to stop the car. Needed to stop the car. She eased up on the accelerator, but to her horror the car didn't slow. If anything, its speed increased.

"Wha... What's wrong?" she stammered.

The stranger was looking at her now, she could feel his dark eyes boring into her. "Haven't you figured it out yet?"

"Figured what out?" Caroline's voice sounded small and weak. She felt ill, the nausea coming in waves. Her foot frantically pumped the brake, but still the car refused to slow.

"Earlier tonight..."

"Earlier tonight? Yes... what?" she demanded.

"Before I found you, you fell asleep at the wheel."

Caroline felt her face flush with shame. "Yes. I almost collided with that other car. I... I was so tired. But how do you know about that? How could you possibly know?"

"I know everything, Caroline. I see everything. I wait in the shadows."

"You wait? Wait for what?"

"I wait to show people the way."

"What are you talking about?"

"You didn't almost collide with that other car, Caroline. You *did* collide with that other car."

As the cold realization began to sink in Caroline shook her head slowly. She took her hands off the wheel, but the car steered itself. It steered itself!

"Who are you? What are you?"

"As I said, you may call me whatever you want. I do believe a popular moniker for me in English is... Death."

"But this can't be happening. I'm on my way to see my father."

"Don't worry, when we arrive at our final destination your father will be there waiting for you."

Christian Saunders, who writes fiction as C.M. Saunders, is a freelance journalist and editor from south Wales. His work has appeared in over 80 magazines, ezines and anthologies worldwide and he has held staff positions at several leading UK magazines ranging from Staff Writer to Associate Editor. His books have been both traditionally and independently published, the latest release being a collection of short fiction called X: Omnibus.

ASPIRIN

Scott Savino

ERIC MORGAN WAS THE one who gave it to me; the little white pill. I don't even do drugs. All I told him was that I had a headache. He asked did I want an aspirin?

Eric and I work together. He has—a problem. It's apparent if you know the signs. The first indicator is how emaciated he is. It's not a nice way to describe a friend, to be sure, but it's the truth. He made himself that way; a wiry frame with wrapping paper for skin. His face is gaunt, all boxy angles of skull. Sometimes there are visible places, sores, where he's picked away too much; Band-Aids for tape to hold the package together. His behavior is strange sometimes and even when he is not high, his eyes are wild and dark.

He knows that I don't take drugs. He knows that my father died from an overdose of opiates. I don't even take aspirin normally; but this headache

103

was just so bad.

We do have a lot in common. Enough for me to be able to overlook his drug abuse. We're both vegan, we both like the same MMORPGs, and we are both transplants here from the same small town. He rarely comes to work high and I try not to judge him for it. Watching my father taught me a little perspective. People don't become addicted to drugs because it's fun.

When he asked me what was wrong I told him, "My head is killing me today. I wish I was dead."

Eric said he had something in his car and offered to run out and get it for me. I reminded him that I don't take any kind of pills normally and I didn't know if I wanted it.

"It's just an aspirin. Don't be a baby."

So I took it.

Yet the headache continued through the day. My boss visited my cubicle around noon. Her style sense may be lacking—given her penchant for wool suits—but her business sense is very forward-thinking. As soon as she realized I wasn't feeling well, she sent me home.

"I can probably make it to the end of the day," I said.

She sighed and crossed her arms, drumming her fingers across the sleeve of that itchy-looking brown suit.

"Now, Scott, you know the rules: Happy employees are productive employees. The ill employees go home and rest because they are not as productive. Come back when you're feeling better."

So I thanked her and headed out the door.

The pain sharpened as I rode down to the parking level, doubling me over. I fell onto the handrail that ran the circumference of the elevator, but managed to right myself and get into my car.

It was after I got home that things started to become odd.

It started as a bruise. I saw it in the mirror as I was getting into the shower.

Was that a trick of the steam on the glass? No. No it wasn't...

On my side was a dark purple and green line about seven inches across; evidence left by the elevator handrail.

As I showered, the sharp pains returned.

I regained consciousness with more bruises of dark violet that radiated with lines of jade and black. I had pulled the towel rack and shower curtain down over me when I passed out. The water was still running hot so I knew I hadn't been out long enough for these types of contusions to have left marks like this.

The strangest thing was that I didn't feel anything. No pain at all. None of the bruises were tender to my touch, and there was no residual throb that I should have felt from the fall after I'd collapsed. Even the headache was gone.

Was it the aspirin?

I'd never suffered fainting spells before, maybe this was the result of that pill.

Maybe Eric had switched what he gave me with something stronger? On purpose? No. He wouldn't have done that. Users don't intentionally dole out their stash.

Maybe the switch was a mistake. Maybe, just maybe, he was high and grabbed the wrong thing. Maybe this was something he didn't intend to give me...

But it didn't make me feel high.

It made me feel nothing. Not even numbness. Just nothing.

After cleaning up the mess, I headed out of the steamy bathroom and into the kitchen. I had not turned the air on when I arrived home but the house was freezing so I checked the thermostat. The current readout on the digital thermometer was either broken or I was getting sick: *84°F*

Chills, I could explain. A fever was something I could deal with. I felt fine, but my curiosity prompted me to grab my thermometer. It's older and takes about two minutes to give a reading. Deciding to multitask, I allowed it to hang from beneath my tongue as I chopped onions to begin making dinner.

The onions did not have their usual pungent aroma, and I chopped with ease until the thermometer beeped with a read-out.

Beep

The display said ERROR.

Maybe it was time for a new one.

I decided to try it again. It was probably foolish to split my attention the way I was. I think that's how I ended up cutting off my left index finger at the second knuckle. I didn't even feel it.

I wrapped my hand in a kitchen towel and put the finger in a bag of ice, then I headed to the emergency room.

◆◆◆

All eyes were on me as I entered through the ER doors. I must have been a sight with that bag of ice and multiple bruises. One woman even gasped. I stumbled up to the admittance desk and they took me and my severed finger to a room immediately.

The doctor seemed confused as he examined my hand and the bruises.

"I'll be right back," he said, and headed out the door. "I'm going to go grab a nurse."

It was something I overheard in his conversation with the nurse in the hall that prompted me to leave the room and sneak out of the hospital. I didn't know what was wrong with me, and he didn't seem to know either.

I did know that I didn't want to be prodded and punctured and opened up so that they could figure it out. I did know that I overheard something about the skin peeling away from my skull. About not bleeding from my hand. About the CDC and quarantine... but the most jarring words from his mouth I heard with unsettling clarity, prompting my abrupt departure.

"He has no blood pressure, no pulse."

I'd seen my share of zombie films and knew all of the implications. I wasn't some bloodthirsty monster out for brains. I just had a headache. I took a pill. This all started with a headache and then I got a bruise...

The more I think about it, I don't think it was aspirin.

Scott Savino lives on Florida's Gulf Coast with his partner Daniel and their dog, Max. His hobbies include long trespassive walks, wandering in the woods after dark, reading, and jumping fearfully from non-aggressive shadows (mostly his own shadow.) His works have been featured in numerous anthologies and updates can be found at http://scottsavino.com/

GHOMESTIC

Laird Long

I WAS OUTSIDE OF A DECREPIT crypt, hugging a tree trunk like a witch hugs a broomstick, when a ghost suddenly floated down out of the night sky and accosted me.

"You're Nancy Dempster? The paranormal legal investigator?"

I grimaced. "Who wants to know?" I whispered, squinting through the vaporous entity at the rusted metal door of the ancient mausoleum beyond.

I was on a stakeout. I'd been hired by a local blood bank to determine if Count Orlov was really disabled and couldn't "collect" plasma on his own, as he claimed, or was actually faking impairment to get free corpuscles from the bank.

"I'm Adele Rochester," the ghost informed me. "I want to hire you to check up on my husband, Rogers. I think he has other haunts."

I would've booed that suggestion out loud if I wasn't in present phantom company. Instead, I said, "I don't handle ghomestics."

"I have to know!" the spirit wailed. "I'll pay you to find out!"

The crypt door creaked open a crack and a pair of glassy yellow eyes peered out, roused to suspicion by the spectral bleatings. The searching orbs spotted me behind the tree, illuminated by the glowing ghost, and the pair of dead eyes darted back down into the gloomy depths of the mausoleum with a clang of the door.

"Great!" I groaned. "All my hours of surveillance—deep-sixed."

"So now you can take my case!"

I shifted my gaze to look at, rather than through, the hovering ghost. She was dressed in ruffles and lace and a hoop skirt that hadn't seen sun since Victorian days. Her face was severe, nose pinched, hair bunned back like a lending librarian's.

"I *have* to find out if Rogers is frequenting haunts other than our own!"

There's more jealousy, spite and bitterness brewing in a ghomestic than in the Wicked Witch's tea cauldron, and anybody getting mixed up in the milieu is liable to get scalded. But I nodded anyway. The blood bank Count Orlov case was the only one I'd had on my docket, and that was clearly done for tonight.

◆◆◆

Adele and her equally lighter-than-dead-air husband, Rogers, haunted a crumbling mansion on the outskirts of town. They'd both been hanged some time past for welcoming weary travellers into their country estate, and then bedding said drifters down in their impromptu cemetery out back. Not the most reputable clients for a licensed para-legal.

But all that was ancient history. When you're in the spook business, you run into a lot of scary clients and hairy situations, and vice versa.

Adele supplied the plan (along with a promise of some silverware she'd stashed away in livelier times). I'd play the role of hapless tourist looking for lodgings for the night, stumble onto the Rochester mansion and stir up the man of the house and his haunting instincts. Then, when Rogers came after me in a flurry of wailing phantasm, I'd run away into the neighbouring woods. She was guessing he would give me the fly-by and keep on going, in which case I was to track him.

Adele said that her husband had flown out of the house in a spirited rage two times before in the past couple of weeks, ghosting after a group of parkouring college kids, and a zombie out on a car-cass rally. Both times, Rogers had taken his sweet time getting back home. He'd claimed he was just out visiting the cemetery where his mother was buried. But his wife was like the Frankenstein monster approached by a lighter salesman; she wasn't buying. And she was coming apart at the seams wanting to know the full truth.

So, I donned a polyester tourist outfit complete with my infra-white camera that looked like a regular camera, and knocked on the slightly unhinged wooden door of the Rochester mansion 'round midnight. No one answered. Just an owl up on the gnarly bare branch of a dead tree.

I pushed the door open. It groaned like my insides. I've been a para-legal going on six years now, but I can still get the heebie-jeebies on a case—especially a ghomestic.

I slipped inside the gloomy house, tiptoed down a dilapidated hallway with just a few shafts of moonlight shining through the rotted walls to guide me. There was more dust in the stale air than at a mummy convention, and cobwebs galore. I sidled left into the spacious living room and shuddered to a stop.

An apparition holding a glow-in-the-dark decanter was standing by the mantelpiece. "Welcome to my home, young lady. Would you care for a drink?"

Despite his courtly manners, he was a pale imitation of a good host. His grin was ghastly, his aim just off the mark. While the decanter that whizzed by my head went right through the wall behind me without breaking, it was my nerves that were shattered.

I exhaled a scream that would've done a horror actress proud, and spun around like a prima ballerina. I raced out of the living room and down the hallway and right through the front door. I was so fleet of frighted foot, in fact, that I had already ducked into the woods to the right of the mansion by the time Rogers Rochester blew out of the haunted house after me.

He screamed at the top of his lungs as he screeched to a stop and spun around, searching the murky landscape for my hunkered form. Then he sailed away down the long, desolate front lawn and out into the great beyond beyond, apparently giving up on his querulous quarry.

My scooter was parked behind a bush. I hopped aboard, keyed the electric motor to life, and then gave chase after the high-flying spectre.

His trail was cold, like any ghoul's, but I could plainly see him up ahead, silhouetted against the night sky. I scooted after him. He zipped right over the huge cemetery that spread out just past the perimeter highway which encircled the city, bypassing any passed friends and/or loved ones. Then he flew over the massive churches that congregated outside city limits, sailed over the river and swooped down onto a cottage that stood on the edge of a slumbering bedroom community.

I had to squeeze every last kilometre per hour out of my scooter's allotted eighty, but I managed to keep pace with Rogers. I skidded to a stealthy stop on the dirt road that bordered the abandoned cottage just in time to witness Rogers vaporize inside the bungalow through the vents in the attic.

I kickstanded my machine and hopped off, unslung my camera and snapped a few pics of the premises—as a framing device for the proof perhaps to follow. Then I inhaled a gasping gulp of courage and slunk over to the cookie-cutter front door of the gingerbread cottage. The breadbox-designed building was approximately the same vintage as the Rochester mansion, but in a little better shape. Termites and spiders hadn't totally redecorated the place yet.

The only sounds were the thumping of my heart, and the thundering of the big rigs out on the highway that led into the city. I gripped my infra-white camera with trembling hands and shouldered the cottage door open with a squeak—mine—and sidled inside the building.

It was as dark and stuffy as a wizard's top hat. I drew another gasping breath, held it (and a hundred dust motes besides), then crept down the short hall and turned into the small parlour to the left. My eyes went wide as my camera lens, as I and it jumped up and shuddered and shuttered respectively.

Rogers Rochester was haunting the parlour—a ghostly woman in his arms!

As I snapped away with the camera, recording the touching love scene, a decayed floorboard suddenly snapped under my foot. My blood ran colder than the Bride of Dracula's on her wedding night. The pair of entwined entities swung their airy heads around and gaped at me.

I got off one more pic for posterity. And then I sprinted for the exit even faster than last time; Rogers on my turned tail, also faster than last time.

"Let me talk to you! I can explain!" he howled.

I broad jumped onto my scooter, and the machine and I went tumbling over onto our sides. Rogers loomed up close, looking scarier than ever.

"I—I caught you white-handed!" I yelped, flat on my back with my scooter on top of me, and one philandering phantom hovering above.

"Adele put you up to this, didn't she?" Rogers asked. "Well, she's got the wrong idea about me, as usual. The woman you saw just now happens to be my sister."

He gestured at the cottage. The femme-phantale he'd been clutching was floating in the doorway, looking out at us on the road.

"Adele has never been able to control her misguided jealousy," Rogers said, trying to convince me.

"Oh, yeah?" I squirmed out from under the scooter and stood up, dusted off the back of my pants.

"Yes. Rachel was poisoned by my wife many years ago, in a similar fit of petulance. She thought I was spending too much time with my own *sister*." Rogers shrugged his broad white shoulders and smiled beguilingly. "I'd appreciate it if you didn't tell my wife that I'm still seeing my sister. She'd make my afterlife a living hell, you understand."

He could be very charming and persuasive, when he wasn't scaring the bejeezus out of you. But I was wary, as befitted my vocation. "What's in it for me?"

Rogers' grin widened. "I happen to know where some gold coins are buried. Very near to their former owners on our estate, as a matter of fact."

The ghost had seen right through me.

◆◆◆

I was hanging from a tree branch like a

115

vampire bat hangs from a tomb rafter, waiting for a witch to take the bait of the child mannequin I'd placed in the copse of trees inside the city park. The witch-baiting gig was a city contract which I'd hoped to milk like a succubus for maximum billable hours at time-and-a-half night rates. Children had been disappearing into the forest, out back of the Hansel and Gretel house in the kiddie amusement park, and a rogue witch was suspected. Suddenly, Adele Rochester swooped down on me like a bad dream, blowing my cover with her cold wind.

"How come you never reported back to me?" she shrieked. "What did you find out about my husband?"

"I didn't find out a thing," I tried to shoo off the angry ghoul. "Your husband was visiting his mother in the cemetery, like he told you."

"Fiddle-faddle!" Adele screeched. "If you don't tell me what you discovered, I'm going to haunt your every sleeping hour!"

I sighed and shifted on the tree branch. And the wooden limb snapped like a werewolf's jaws. I dropped out of the tree and bounced down on the turf below.

And before I could shake the stars out of my eyes, Adele had zipped over to my fallen infra-white camera and was flooding it with her vapour, trying to see what lay stored within. I jumped to my feet and rushed over before she really fogged up the works. Infra-whites with teleghopic lenses don't come cheap.

I reluctantly showed Adele the pictures of her husband and the other woman, still in my camera's memory. Unfortunately, the wispy lady's disposition didn't improve any at what she saw.

"That's not Rogers' sister!" she wailed, loud enough to wake the undead. "That's his former mistress, Rochelle! I'm going to kill that man!"

She streaked off into the night to wreak vengeance upon her adulterous apparition of a hubby, no doubt to try to destroy his spirit.

I gave my woozy head another shake, then brushed pine needles off my black shirt and jeans, knowing for sure I wasn't catching any child-snatching witches that night. And knowing for certain, as well, that I would now be visited by another angry ghost on another darkened night; Rogers Rochester, looking for spectral retribution for my double-dealing, and specifically repayment of his golden hush money (which I'd already spent.)

That's why I try to make it a rule to never get involved in ghomestics. They're just too scary.

Long pounds out fiction in all genres. Big guy, sense of humour. Writing credits include: Blue Murder Magazine, Hardboiled, Bullet, Sherlock Holmes Mystery Magazine, Mystery Weekly Magazine, Woman's World, that's life!, The Weekly News, The Forensic Examiner, Cricket, You, Hooked, and stories in the anthologies The Prison Compendium, The Mammoth Book of New Comic Fantasy, The Mammoth Book of Jacobean Whodunits, The Mammoth Book of Perfect Crimes

and Impossible Mysteries, and New Canadian Noir.

THROUGH THE GLASS DARKLY

Margery Bayne

THE MERMAID WAS SLIMY.

Her skin was sallow and her body stretched-looking, long and thin. But the worst were her eyes—pupil-less, milky white pearls. Eyes that stared Ariana down through the aquarium's six-inch thick glass.

She had remained hidden the entire party, much to Max's ever jaw-tightening irritation. Very few people in the world owned merpeople, because very few had been captured alive since their first discovery in the deepest, darkest reaches of the ocean just three years ago.

Last year there had been a shark in the tank for Max to show off and for the guests to admire. Last year was also when Ariana had first met Max, although she had been dressed in a catering uniform instead of Marchesa.

Ariana stroked her thumb along the underside of her engagement ring.

Still staring at her, the mermaid lifted her hand—her webbed fingers as spindly as the rest of her—and pressed her palm against the glass.

Ariana glanced over her shoulder. The room was empty except for the tables now stripped of their linens. The staff had already cleaned up and gone.

Near the closing of the party, Max had told her, "Stay here, I'll be right back," before he slipped away to his office with a business associate. How long ago had that been? She couldn't even wear a bra with this dress, let alone find somewhere to tuck away her phone.

Max had acquired his new pet this past Friday, during Ariana's week long out-of-town visit to see her mother. She had only arrived back at the mansion this afternoon. This was her first time seeing the mermaid, and she hated the creature and the fact she'd have to see her here in the entrance hall, and in Max's office, and the sitting room, and the den, all rooms that shared another side of this aquarium as one of their walls. Max had designed this layout himself.

Without knowing why, Ariana raised her hand and laid it on the glass opposite the mermaid's. The glass was a gulf between them, but it was almost like touching.

As she stared back, as their hands didn't quite touch, Ariana found she couldn't breathe. She tried to suck in a breath, but it wouldn't go down her throat. Her lungs burned and a panicked notion passed through her mind, the last thing she would see were those horrible, milky eyes.

"There she is."

Those three words broke the spell. Ariana jerked back. If Max hadn't been right there at her elbow to steady her, she would've toppled over in her heels.

The mermaid backflipped in the water and swam away, disappearing behind a decorative rock structure.

Max sighed. Ariana felt the puff of his breath on her exposed neck.

"Been like this since I got her," he said, wrapping an arm around Ariana's waist and pulling her tight to his side. Her breathing had returned as if it had never been absent, like there hadn't just been some noose around her neck.

"Well, who likes to be looked at all the time?" Ariana said, as if the whole moment with the mermaid hadn't just happened. She was good at pushing the horror down her throat and smiling.

It hadn't just happened, right? It was all the result of too much champagne and jet lag. It was some passing asthma attack.

"You, by the way, look divine." He turned her towards him and kissed her harder than she liked. She'd have to excuse it; she'd been away for a week after all.

Although they were alone, Ariana couldn't ignore the lingering discontent of the mermaid's presence.

"Let's go to bed," she whispered, with all of its implications. The aquarium wall did not extend to

121

the bedroom, thank god. She had limits.

Ariana's eyes blinked open, as calm as waking up, confused to find herself staring at the gym ceiling, the upper half of her body cradled in Max's arms, both of them on the floor.

"Are you alright?" he said.

"What…?" Ariana said, voice wispy. She'd wanted to get out a whole sentence, but she gave up with just a word. Her heart was pounding so fierce in her chest; she felt breathless.

Breathless. She blinked, her memories reforming out of her confusion.

"You were running and you just passed out," Max said.

But it was more than that. She'd been running on the treadmill, yes, like every morning workout, while Max lifted weights. Halfway through her iPod's workout playlist, a dizziness had overcome her. She couldn't suck in air fast enough, and then, not at all. She had tried to slap at the stop button, she remembered, but her arms had been so weak and useless, her vision so fuzzy.

Here she was, on the floor, because she had temporarily lost the ability to breathe.

Max sat her up. "I'm calling Dr. Cosman."

"No, I feel fine," Ariana said. Insisted over and again, but Max called anyway, and she was made to wait in the sitting room for the doctor's arrival.

Dr. Cosman was one of those celebrity doctors, paid well for house calls and discretion. As he checked her blood pressure, she gave him all the excuses she had given herself—jetlag, hangover, she hadn't slept well.

Max left the room to get ready for work once Dr. Cosman assured him Ariana was out of immediate danger. Alone, he sat down on the ottoman directly in front of her. "Have you been eating?" he asked.

Ariana gritted her teeth. "Yes."

He stared at her, as if trying to read a lie. "Take it easy," he said, standing, "until I get the results of the blood tests."

She passed her morning in the armchair, frustrated and trembling, chilly in her sweat-damp workout clothes, a caffeine headache growing behind her eyes.

A ghost floated by the corner of her vision.

She startled, letting out an embarrassing little shout that there was no one around to hear but her.

When she looked, she realized it wasn't a ghost though. It was the mermaid hovering on the other side of the aquarium wall.

As Ariana watched, the mermaid raised her hand and laid it against the glass.

She stumbled up from her seat and fled to the bedroom, and cocooned under the blankets where she couldn't be seen.

◆◆◆

Ariana awoke, fitfully, mid-afternoon, gasping for air.

She got out of bed and hobbled into the en

suite, splashing water from the sink onto her face. Asthma. Allergies. She never had those problems before, but they could be new, right?

Psychosomatic? Was she losing it? She stared at her face in the mirror, hair in disarray, face blotchy and makeup-less. This wouldn't do.

She stripped out of her clothes and stepped into the shower. Before Max got home, she made herself up like they were going out tonight. If she looked good, maybe she'd feel better. At the least, Max would appreciate it.

Max came home angry, some business deal gone wrong. Ariana had stopped trying to understand and offer advice months ago. She had been told she couldn't possibly understand; so she let him rant, nothing more than a sounding board, telling herself that this was a privilege. She was the only one allowed to see the great Max Rhodes so unraveled.

He slammed a hand down on the table and she didn't even flinch. It was like she was hearing the whole thing through water.

When Ariana got home from a visit with the wedding planner, where high-intensity decisions like chocolate or lemon cake were made, the mermaid was waiting for her.

"Are you obsessed with me?" Ariana said, trying to sound indifferent and mildly miffed, like she might be able to convince herself with her own act.

She took her jacket to the hall closet. Her heels echoed too loudly on the Grecian tile floor, the only sound in the large entrance hall.

When she turned around, the mermaid was still there, waiting, staring, palm flat against the glass.

Ariana fisted her hands at her side, acrylic nails—she was a biter—digging into the soft flesh of her palms.

"I'm not afraid of you," Ariana said, although certainly the mermaid couldn't hear across the room, through the glass, and through the water. Of course Ariana was only saying this for herself. That was the only sensible thing.

"It would be insane to be afraid of you." She forced a step forward; it was easier to be less afraid at a distance. "You can't touch me through that glass. You're the one trapped here. I'm free to come and go as I please." A few more steps. Soon, she was in an arm's reach of the glass, nearly nose-to-nose with the creature, pallid hair floating about her head like a halo.

Ariana found it hard to breathe, but different from before, not suffocating yet. This was born of her own fear, a corset type of non-breathing, like there wasn't enough room in her chest. The other times—at first touch, on the treadmill, from her nap—it had been like her throat had been closing in until her lungs burned from the lack of oxygen.

Ariana raised her shaking hand. "It's nothing," she said, and pressed her hand opposite the mermaid's.

And nothing. Blissfully nothing. She panted in relief, taking in all the air in the world.

125

It felt sharper than ever before; an invisible hand wrapping itself around her neck and squeezing with an unyielding force.

She should've been afraid. She should've stayed afraid.

The mermaid dropped her hand from the glass and Ariana was released. She tottered back, fell on her butt, tried to stand too fast, twisted her ankle in her shoe, and landed hard again, this time on her kneecap. Pain shot through her entire leg.

She didn't get back up.

◆◆◆

Max found her, sobbing on the floor.

"You have to get rid of that thing," she said when he asked her what was wrong.

"What thing?"

"That!" She jabbed her finger at the tank, where the mermaid was swimming restlessly, back and forth, but not away.

"The mermaid?"

"It's... It's…"

"I know it's a little… well, she's not exactly out of Disney, is she? But what happened? She gave you a startle?"

"No, not a startle. It's evil. It's vile—"

"Come on now." He hauled her to her feet. She wobbled, unable to put her full weight on her sprained ankle. He stood behind her, braced his hands on her shoulders and started moving her towards the tank. "Look. It can't hurt you."

"Max. No." She didn't have the strength to

prevent him from pushing her forward on her strongest day. Right now, she was injured and distraught.

It didn't stop her from pressing her good foot into the floor, from flailing against his hold, trying to get out of his grip.

"Stop it! I said no."

"You weren't afraid of the shark, but you're afraid of this."

She was going to die. If he didn't stop, she was going to die.

They were too close.

She flung her head back.

"Christ!" His voice echoed and he dropped his hold. Ariana barely managed to stay standing at the sudden release on her weak ankle. Her shoes had been kicked off in her struggle.

Max clutched his face, blood flowing between his fingers.

The back of her skull had collided with his nose.

"What's wrong with you?" he asked, angry and muffled, and he stomped off to the bathroom before she could say a thing.

◆◆◆

"Are you having a nervous breakdown? Is it wedding planning stress? Is it your mother?"

Dr. Cosman had come and gone, fixed up Max's nose. Both of his eyes were bruised.

Ariana sat on the bed beside him, feeling numb. No, not numb. She felt too awful to be numb.

"It can't be easy to fly halfway across the

127

country to spend time with a woman who can't remember you."

Ariana inhaled. This was one time she wished she could stop breathing.

"Do you need to see someone?" The implication, a head doctor.

"It was an accident. I didn't mean to hurt you."

"I know that. But you've been acting strange…"

"Jetlag," she said. "I haven't been able to sleep."

Only later would she notice the bruises ringing her own arms from Max's fingers.

"Why are you making me do this?" Ariana said, as they rode up in the cramped utility elevator.

"You need to get over this fear," Max replied. His black eyes looked worse this morning. She could just imagine the press speculation.

The elevator doors slid open to the narrow concrete platform that ringed the top opening of the giant aquarium. Max had a marine biologist on payroll who was usually the only one to come up here.

Ariana had come so far, from the Midwest to New York City, from paycheck-to-paycheck to lap of luxury. She couldn't lose it all now because she was *crazy*.

A dark thought betrayed her, at least get married first. At least have a divorce settlement to land back on when he inevitably gets tired of you.

As soon as Ariana stepped out on the platform, the elevator doors slid shut behind her, Max still inside. Ariana jammed the down button, but the elevator didn't reopen. She slammed a fist against the doors.

"Max, you bastard," she shouted. Her voice echoed.

She turned to look at the tank, back pressed to the elevator doors. If she pretended, it just looked like a swimming pool.

A dark shape moved in the depths.

"Oh no, oh no, oh no." She closed her eyes, pressing harder against the doors. "I'm seeing things. I'm just seeing things."

She opened her eyes. The shape was bigger.

And it only grew bigger with every beat of her heart that passed, until it was no longer a shape, but a defined figure, distorted by the water's ripples.

The mermaid was coming for her.

Then, about four yards out into the tank, her head popped above the surface. Her unsettling pearl eyes were set on Ariana.

The mermaid began to swim towards her.

Ariana jammed her thumb again at the down button, but the elevator doors remained shut and she could hear no rumble of it moving. Max had maybe locked it downstairs. It didn't matter. The elevator wasn't coming; the mermaid was. She was stuck. There was no escape.

And still, the mermaid swam closer, zigzagging towards Ariana like a predator teasing its assuredly-trapped prey.

She understood now. It had all been an omen

leading to this; the day the mermaid would drown her.

Ariana slid down the length of elevator doors—pleading, praying, to the elevator, to anything, to the mermaid, for respite.

The mermaid stopped about an arm's length back in the water from the edge of platform. If she came right up, she could so easily reach Ariana, grab her ankle, pull her under. There was nowhere to retreat.

The mermaid raised her arm from the water, extended, hand aloft and just waited there. Ariana blinked. This was how she had always waited for Ariana to come to her.

Beyond reason, Ariana felt herself begin to move.

On her knees, she reached out and took the mermaid's hand.

The mermaid's hand was uncomfortably moist and her grip strong. Ariana winced. Not from any pain, but in anticipation of it. After a second, none came. She opened her eyes.

But relief didn't last long as the familiar choking sensation around her neck once again overcame her, stronger and sharper than before.

Images, both dreamlike and vivid, flittered through her mind's eye. That invisible hand choking her wasn't invisible. It was real and flesh. And it was Max's. Max—face contorted in rage— above her, squeezing the life out of her, her lungs burning, her throat aching, her body going from flailing to limp, being pressed, being held, under water...

The mermaid let go. Ariana's empty hand hung in the air as she coughed in new air. She blinked tears of pain from her vision.

"What was that?" Ariana asked. The mermaid cocked her head and did nothing more. "What was that?" she yelled, but the mermaid either couldn't hear or didn't care or was torturing her worse than ever.

The elevator grunted, gears grinding loudly, as it came back to life, moving. The mermaid dove back under the water.

"Come back!"

She stood. This was just another one of the mermaid's tricks. Messing with her head, with her marriage anxieties. Max would never...

Ariana touched her sleeve where underneath were hidden the ring of bruises.

On the ride down the elevator, Max said, "Did you see the mermaid really wasn't anything to be afraid of?"

Ariana couldn't look him in the face, could only look at his hands, loose at his sides.

She typed "How do mermaids communicate" into the Google search bar and sifted through an insane number of results before she found a shoddily translated article from Japan. Tokyo had a pair of merpeople in a public aquarium, the only two in the world that weren't kept in ego-stroking private collections.

Turned out that merpeople, despite their

humanoid half, differed from humans in lacking vocal cords. They couldn't speak or make meaningful noise. Their natural habitats were too dark for a visual language like sign language. Biologists theorized they used some kind of coded touch, based on their observations of the pair in captivity.

That was it. No answers. No explanations.

Ariana pressed the flat of her two palms together.

But the merpeople touched. They touched, like Ariana and her mermaid.

♦♦♦

Ariana lifted her eyes from her dinner plate. The steak, the broccoli, the baked potato, cut up and rearranged, all still there.

"How did your first wife die?" she asked.

"What kind of question is that?" Max said, after he finished chewing and swallowing.

"I always thought it would be something we talked about before the wedding. That you've been married before." Once she had harbored fleeting, romantic dreams of "you're the one who taught me how to love again" type confessions, of being more important than pretty.

"It's public record," he said, sawing out the next chunk from his steak. "You could look it up."

"I didn't want to look it up," Ariana said. It might've been important news in New York society back before she lived here, but Max wasn't so famous that his life saturated pop culture beyond that. "I wanted…" Him to tell her, freely. This wasn't that either.

"She drowned. In the bathtub. Accident." He lifted his glass of red wine, matched by the chef for this meal. "You happy now?"

She googled this too: "How did Melanie Rhodes die?"

The news reports corroborated Max's story, but added this detail: autopsy showed she had taken sleeping pills—a valid prescription of hers—before her death. Investigators ruled it an accident, said she fell asleep in the bath and slipped under the water. A painless death, but tragic, for the woman who had been behind the man all the way, as he built his fortune from a one-bedroom apartment all the way to the top of the world. The man everyone wanted to be, or be with.

Ariana clicked on images of Melanie, a round-faced brunette, and touched the pixelated images with her fingertips, wondering what would've become of her if she'd still been alive. Would Ariana still be here, in Max's house? Would Ariana have been the "other woman"? Was Ariana the natural replacement in the saga of rich men and their trade-off in wives?

Melanie, homely and solid, never even stood a chance.

♦♦♦

133

When Ariana woke up that night from dreams of drowning, it was so quiet. Max hadn't stirred, and was snoring beside her. She settled back into her pillow with a sense of serenity, bizarre and detached, not afraid of sleep and what dreams it might bring. She could wake up from dreams. It was reality that was harder to extricate herself from.

◆◆◆

She drew designs—swirls and hearts and little rings—in the surface of the water, waiting. It took only a few minutes for the mermaid to arrive, breaking the surface closer this time. The mermaid came close, propped her elbows up on the edge of the platform, like children do at the pool.

"You've been trying to tell me something this whole time," Ariana said. "Is that it?"

But the mermaid could give her no verbal answer. Ariana knew this now, scientifically.

She gulped, reached out, and touched two fingertips to the flesh of the mermaid's arm. The mermaid tilted her head. Could the mermaid see her, really? She was a creature of the darkest parts of the ocean. Were her eyes even made for seeing? Had all the ominous staring all this time, been Ariana projecting?

Ariana shut her eyes, didn't speak, and thought of the suffocation the mermaid had shown her all these times, of Max, of Melanie, of what she thought the mermaid had been trying to tell her. She didn't think these thoughts in words, or tried not to. She tried to think the way the mermaid had conveyed thought to her—in images, in sensations.

She wasn't sure if it was working, but she tried, and the mermaid didn't pull away. Somehow, during all this concentration, the bubble that was caught in Ariana's chest came out as a sob.

"I don't know what to do."

Just as she was about the drop her hand, the mermaid caught her wrist.

Later she walked out of the elevator, back onto the main floor, with a plan.

◆◆◆

A text on her phone read, "Remember. Dress Fitting! 11 sharp!" followed by the address. Ariana was waiting for a response from someone else.

Her phone chimed, a new text, "On my way up now."

The elevator doors slide open and Max stepped out. "What is it?" he asked, tugging at his sleeves. "Why're we up here?"

"I wanted to show you something," Ariana said, and pointed into the water. "Look." Not far below the surface, the mermaid was swimming a figure eight.

Max leaned over the edge. That's when, with his balance precarious, Ariana amassed all her strength and pushed.

He toppled into the water. The mermaid did her part, kept him from swimming, from climbing back out. She dragged him down, down, down.

Ariana pressed the elevator button, the water behind her settling from the splash, the intertangled blob of Max and the mermaid growing smaller as they sunk deeper. The elevator opened.

For the sake of appearances, Ariana went to her dress fitting.

◆◆◆

Some people will say, The fiancée did it, for the money.

Some people will say, No way, look at her, she's tiny. Plus, she only got a couple hundred thousand. If she waited a few more months, married the guy first, she would've had billions.

Police investigators will say, It's unfortunate that there were no cameras inside the house, but Mr. Rhodes was known for his privacy. We can only follow the facts. We don't have evidence to support that Mr. Rhodes' fiancée, Ariana Stowe, took part in his death.

A tabloid headline will read, Killer Mermaid Murders Billionaire. Who's Next?

Ariana will say, in an interview two weeks after the funeral, one week after the investigation was closed, It's tragic. I'll never get to wear my wedding dress. I'll never get to say my vows. But I've come to a decision in regard to the mermaid. I don't hate her for what she did. She's a wild creature, forced out of her habitat and everything she knows, into a cage. I mean, aquarium. She lashed out. That's why I'm advocating for the mermaid to be returned to the ocean. It's the natural thing… Oh, what's next for me? I'm moving back to Ohio, to take care of my mother. It's where I belong. I just want to live a quiet life, away from the cameras. I never fit in here anyway.

Margery Bayne is a librarian by day and a writer by night. She enjoys the literary and speculative, and is a published short story author and an aspiring novelist. In 2012, she graduated from Susquehanna University with a BA in Creative Writing and is currently pursuing a Masters of Library Science. She'll read anything from children's chapter book to YA graphic novels to mainstream bestsellers as long as it has a good story. In her time not spent reading or writing, she enjoys origami, running, and being an aunt. She is a native of the greater Baltimore area of Maryland where she still currently resides. More about her and her writing can be found at http://www.margerybayne.com or on facebook @writermargerybayne.

TRICK OR TREAT

Dianna Duncan

SURE, MY PROFESSION IS dangerous. Lots of professions are dangerous. Granted, some are more dangerous than others. If you stop and think about it, even a librarian could be considered a dangerous profession with the possibility of the loss of limb or life from an infected paper cut. Or a book could fall off the shelf and hit her on the head, but that is obviously a bit far-fetched.

My job didn't used to be considered a dangerous one. In fact, it was downright boring. Not too much to write home about if you are a dentist. How does this sound?

Dear family, I cleaned some more teeth today, filled a cavity, pulled out a wisdom tooth, and had to deal with more different kinds of bad breath than I want to think about.

Aside from the breath part, the highest level of danger would be an accidental bite from a patient, but that is why dentists shove lots of cotton in patients' mouths.

See? It is just boring with a capital B. On top of that, nobody, and I mean *nobody* ever wants to go see a dentist. While it is obviously not exciting, it is one of the most hated professions around. In fact, it is the source of extreme fear for many.

That was my life and profession until just over a year ago. Actually, I remember the exact day—it was Halloween last year. To any self-respecting dentist, Halloween is a terrible holiday. I have had some of my worst nightmares come true after Halloween. Why, oh why do parents allow their children to run around the streets begging for candy, and then allow them to go crazy eating it? I can think of no other holiday event that is so dangerous.

I did try passing out toothbrushes instead of candy one year but that was obviously a bad choice. I spent hours the next morning picking toothbrushes out of the bushes in front of my house. Not wanting to participate in contributing to the delinquency of minors through the insanity of providing excessive sugar and encouraging subsequent promotion of tooth decay, I tried to do anything I could to make sure that I was not home all night on Halloween. The best place to hide from the trick-or-treaters is my office.

So there I was last Halloween, sequestered in my office and drinking a glass of wine—It is better for your teeth than eating candy—when I heard a strange scratching at the door. I figured some poor pooch was spooked by the trick-or-treaters. I am not really a dog person, but I decided to let it into the safe haven of my office. When I opened the door, I thought someone was playing a trick on me. A tall, pale person in a black cape stood there.

"Let me guess, you are Count Dracula?" I just couldn't keep the sarcasm out of my voice.

His eyes glowed red as he glared at me and slightly raised an eyebrow. "Dentist?" His voice was low, almost melodic. It stopped me in my tracks and sent a chill down my spine. "Dentist? You are a dentist, yes?"

I realized that I was staring at him with my mouth hanging open. I briefly wondered how he had known I was in my office. "Oh, yes. I am sorry. I was just startled to see you at the door. Yes, I am a dentist. Can I do something for you? Do you need a dentist?"

"I realize that this may sound strange considering… well, considering my line of work and what I do with my teeth, but yes, I do need a dentist." He smiled, displaying strangely pointed teeth. I stepped back into the office and put my hand to my own throat. "Please," he said, "do not be afraid. I declare peace between us. I mean you no harm. Can you assist me?" He held his hands out, palms up.

The next moment was the most pivotal in my life. A million different thoughts ran through my head as I stood there. A vampire stood in front of me asking me to check his teeth. If the stories you hear are true, these teeth have been puncturing the necks of generations of people for many hundreds of years. I wondered how safe I really was with an actual live vampire standing in front of me.

Actually, I guess the word *live* really isn't an appropriate word to use when speaking about vampires, but that is not the point here. I don't know if *trust* was exactly the feeling that I felt when he held his hands out, but there was something there. Maybe it was the thought of the challenge and reaching out for new horizons and events. Maybe I just decided it was time for a change in my life. Regardless, I agreed to perform dentistry on a vampire.

It was a long night and I learned a lot about vampires. Since I was initially apprehensive about putting my hands in his mouth, I took the x-rays first. Except that I discovered x-rays don't work— there really are no images on either mirrors or pictures. My first clue about that was when I put my mirror tool into his mouth and didn't see anything. No, really, nothing at all. After that I didn't even bother examining the x-ray. One glance told me I wouldn't find anything out by looking at the blank film.

He decided that he did not want any numbing medication or anything for pain. I think it probably had something to do with the terminology and his aversion to being stabbed.

Yes, I used lots of cotton in his mouth. He may have declared peace with me but all of those sharp teeth made me decide to be extra cautious.

To sum that appointment up, teeth are basically still teeth and a broken tooth is still painful no matter whose mouth you are talking about. One more note about the procedure—his breath was about as nasty as any breath I have ever smelled. I am not sure if it was something about him being so old or if perhaps it was from having so many different blood types in his mouth. That is not something that I want to spend time dwelling on. I was grateful for the face mask that I wore since it seemed to mute the stench a bit.

The Count was a satisfied patient. A simple crown took care of both his chipped tooth and the pain from the exposed nerve.

I could have gone back to being just a boring dentist again, except for one thing. They say that word-of-mouth is the best advertisement. In this case, when the mouth that is doing the advertising has lots of sharp teeth it probably carries even more weight.

Since that night, my new patients have included three more vampires, two witches, and four werewolves. One zombie also stopped by, but we mutually decided that the teeth that were falling out of his mouth were the least of his problems. With no solid gums to work with, the only possible option would have been dentures and he decided that would be more trouble than it was worth.

The stories about their ancient gold are also true. So true, in fact, that I no longer have daytime office hours. I just work a couple of days each week from ten at night until four in the morning.

What I first thought was a trick, turned out to be a treat, and now I have a monstrously thriving practice!

❀

Dianna lives in Illinois, just the other side of the river from St Louis, with her husband of just over 30 years, and her two cats. While she has previously dabbled in writing short stories and poetry, this is her first submission for publication. She has enjoyed reading the other "Read on the Run" anthologies and is both proud and excited to be included in his one. In addition, she is now eagerly looking forward to the prospect of reworking and completing earlier writings.

ALWAYS PARIS

R. J. Meldrum

I SAT IN THE KITCHEN, watching the cup of coffee in front of me go cold. There was a thump from above, then the noise of someone descending the stairs. Jess had decided to stay over, sleeping in her old bed.

"Morning Dad. You okay?"

I winced. I knew what she meant, but still.

"Sorry, stupid question."

"That's alright. Yes, I am, as much as I can be."

Jess caught me glancing at the print on the wall above the fridge; a faded photograph of the Eiffel Tower. It'd been Jo's favorite picture; she'd had it for most of her life.

"It was always Paris for Mom, wasn't it?"

I smiled, feeling tears well.

"Yes, it was always Paris."

"It's a shame she never got to go."

I nodded, unable to speak.

144

"Do you want a fresh cup?"

"No thanks. Help yourself if you want one."

She did, sitting beside me on the kitchen island.

"We had some good times here, didn't we? Christmases. Birthdays."

"We did."

"Any plans for today?"

"I think I'll just take things easy."

"I think you should. It's been tough for you."

"It's been tough for all of us."

I first met Jo at frosh week, 1985. I'd been accepted at a university in the city. I was a nervous, shy eighteen-year-old; a boy from the suburbs. My parents dropped me off; Dad shook my hand in a manly way while Mom stifled tears. I unloaded my suitcase from the car and watched them drive off. I was on my own for the first time in my life.

My roommate was Peter. He'd arrived the day before. On the second day we went to a party. It was held in Jo's dorm room. There were about twenty of us crammed into the tiny bedroom she shared with her roommate. I didn't know anyone except Peter, who quickly disappeared. I ended up shoved against Jo, near the window.

"Is this your room?"

"Yes."

I noticed a picture of the Eiffel Tower. A plain black and white photograph, stuck on the wall above one of the beds.

"Have you ever been?" I said, pointing.

145

"No, never. That's my photo. I take it everywhere with me. I've always wanted to go. It's an ambition of mine."

"I'd love to visit Europe one day. See all the history."

"It's just Paris for me. I've always loved Paris."

That simple conversation was the start of it.

♦♦♦

Jess had to leave, Dan and the baby couldn't be left alone for too long. Dan was a nice guy, but he was still a little out of his depth with his new daughter. I understood, I'd felt the same way when Jess had been born. She kissed me on the cheek, a worried expression on her face. I did my best to smile. It wasn't fair to her, losing a parent at twenty-seven, three months after the birth of her own child. I felt bad for her, not just because of Jo, but because of the decision I'd made; I knew it was going to get worse for her. I hoped she would be okay. I hoped she could forgive me.

After she left, I wandered around the house, unsettled. It was far too quiet. I walked into our bedroom. The room where she died. The room where I no longer slept. Looking into her closet, I saw Jo's clothes just as they had been when she was alive. I guessed I'd have to do something about them; I couldn't just leave them. They could go to Goodwill or something.

I thought back to the funeral. It had been ghastly. Everyone had been so nice, so considerate.

I envied the people who got to come to the service, give their condolences and then leave, returning to normality. Having to stand there and accept their best wishes was the worst experience of my life. Well, perhaps the second worst. Watching her die topped the list. I was selfish, I always hoped I would die first.

♦♦♦

1989. We graduated on the same day. Our families sat together in the audience, clapping and cheering. We'd been together since that first party. Our lives after graduation were going to be intertwined, there was no way we would separate. Jo had accepted a place at a teaching college; it had always been her plan to teach high school. I enrolled in a Master's program at a nearby university. We got an apartment together, scraping by on a tiny amount of money. Our first home.

That year was tough; even though we'd pretty much lived together during our time as undergraduates, we could always head back to our rooms when we felt the tension build. Not so easy when we were sharing the same space. We had some fights during that first year, but nothing that we couldn't recover from. I remember lying in bed holding her after one of our arguments. It was April and the academic year was nearly over.

"We should take a break in the summer. Get away."

"We can't afford it."

"I've got those bonds from Grandma Smith.

I've had them years, might as well see what they're worth. You could finally get to see Paris."

Jo rolled over and stared at me.

"We might need that money for something else."

♦♦♦

The phone rang, shattering the silence in the house. It was the crematorium. Her ashes were ready; the person on the line asked what I wanted to do with them. I said I'd have to think about it. They suggested the memorial garden, but Jo hadn't wanted that. She wanted them to be scattered. But where? I glanced at the picture of the Eiffel Tower. It was so obvious I was surprised I hadn't thought of it before.

♦♦♦

Jess was born on the seventh of November 1990. She was the reason we couldn't go to Paris that first summer. Grandma Smith's bonds were sold to pay for all the baby stuff we needed. Jo's parents were concerned her studies would be put on hold, that her career would suffer, and I agreed with them. I withdrew from my Master's program while Jo continued her studies. My parents were upset about my decision, but I was content. It made sense, Jo was far more likely to get a job when she graduated and once the baby was a bit older I could continue my studies.

While Jess slept during the day, I pottered

around, cleaning and tidying. After a couple of months, I decided to write some short stories. This was something I'd done since I was a kid. Jo encouraged me to submit some. I was surprised when they were accepted. Success followed success and by the time Jess was three, I'd had a novel published. Jo was happy teaching and I continued to stay at home to write and look after little Jess.

With the advance from my second novel, we put a deposit down on a house, the house where I still lived. The house that had been our home. We took small vacations, but most of our spare cash went into the house. We both forgot about Paris for a few years.

◆◆◆

I decided to pick up Jo's ashes by myself. I knew Jess would want to come, but it was something I had to do alone. The crematorium was cool and calm. So were the staff. They mentioned the memorial garden again. I thanked them, but refused. They passed me a cardboard box. I opened it and removed the contents. The urn was grey and surprisingly light. I tried not to think about what was inside. Part of me knew the cold, hard facts. The ashes inside were the ground up bones of my wife; the fire from the cremation would have left no flesh, no skin. I felt no emotion when I held the container, there was no link here to the strong, vivacious woman I had loved. I put it back in the box and left the crematorium.

149

Jess's car was sitting in the driveway when I got back. She was tearful.

"I phoned the crematorium. They told me you had just left."

"It was something I had to do myself."

There was no answer for that. Jess picked up the box.

"This isn't Mom."

"I know."

"I wish she'd been buried. I would have somewhere to grieve."

"You know she didn't want that."

"I know."

"What are you going to do with them?"

"There is only one place."

"Paris?"

"Paris."

◆◆◆

The years flew by. It was suddenly 2003. I concentrated on writing, while Jo focused on her job. She started to complain about a pain in her stomach. She was head of the English department at her school and worked incredibly hard. We both put the pain down to stress. After three months, blood appeared in her urine. She went to see her doctor.

It was stomach cancer.

I remember the shock I felt when I first heard those words. This sounded like a death sentence. I could see Jo felt the same. The doctor was less sure, she thought the prognosis was good. It had been caught early. It was treatable.

Jo took leave from work and spent her days either in hospital or at home. Three months passed. The doctor reported back. The chemo was working. It was so hard to see her bald and thin, but it had to be done if she was going to recover.

I have little coherent memory of that time. It was a blur of moving between the house and hospital. Daily reports to parents. Fielding phone calls from concerned colleagues and friends. I told my agent I wouldn't be completing my third novel for a while. She was understanding, giving me some time. She told me the first two novels were coming out in paperback, so there was no rush for the third.

The cancer went into remission after six months. I remember the day we were told the good news. Jo lay in our big bed, looking tiny. She held my hand.

"I guess someone has plans for me. Decided it wasn't time."

"I guess."

"The doc says it's gone. The mass has shrunk to nothing."

"I know. It's amazing news."

She frowned.

"It could come back, you know."

"Better not to think like that. Let's decide it won't."

"Okay boss."

I kissed her on the forehead and left her to sleep.

151

I decided I didn't want anything to go wrong, so I checked with customs. Apparently, it wasn't a big issue. Verification from the crematorium. A fee. The appropriate forms were filled out and stamped.

Jess wanted to come, but I wouldn't let her. Jo's last journey had to be with just me. Finish as we'd started.

"Where are you going to scatter them?"

"I'm not sure. Into the Seine perhaps. Or from the top of the Eiffel Tower. I'll take some time to decide. I think I'll know when the time is right."

"Okay, but keep in contact. Let me know."

Her brow was furrowed with worry. I wondered if she had guessed.

September 2015 found Jo appointed as Assistant Principal of her school. It also found me with my fifth novel published. Jess was newly married and settled. Everything was going well, but it wasn't to last. I was about to go on a book tour when Jo dropped the bombshell. There was blood in her urine again. I imagined a thousand different reasons why this was happening, but we both knew.

This time the prognosis wasn't good. After being in remission for years, the cancer was back. It was no longer just in her stomach; it had spread to her lungs and pancreas. There was nothing they could do except treat the symptoms. Jo decided not to allow herself to be admitted to hospital.

"They can give me painkillers, but I'm not having tubes stuck in me anymore. Last time was bad enough. I won't have chemo. It won't make any difference."

I had never seen her so alive, so adamant that she wouldn't go through it all again. Her mind was clear and I had no option but to support her. Jess cried buckets when she found out, desperately trying to persuade her mother to try every treatment possible, just to keep herself alive. Jess had just found out she was pregnant.

I wasn't privy to the conversation that occurred between mother and daughter. All I know is that Jess entered our bedroom, sure she would convince Jo to accept chemotherapy to prolong her life long enough to get to know her first grandchild. But when Jess left, eyes red from crying, she had accepted the inevitable. Such is the bond between mother and daughter.

Jo lasted ten months, long enough for her to meet little Amy, her granddaughter. I would like to say that Jo didn't suffer during those months, but that would be a lie.

The day she died was a clear, bright morning. I had slept on the sofa for a few nights. On that morning, the one I remember with utter clarity, I rose and entered the bedroom quietly. She seemed to be asleep. I stroked her forehead, thinking how peaceful she looked. She was cold.

I stepped off the plane at Charles De Gaulle.

153

I'd transported Jo in my hand luggage and could feel her bumping against my leg as I carried the backpack.

"Well, Jo, you've finally made it to Paris. I'm just sorry it had to be like this. We should have come here... before. I'm sorry."

I expected to feel a sense of fulfillment, of a promise kept, but I felt nothing. I wished Jo was here with me. I headed to the shuttle buses ferrying passengers into the city.

I'd rented an apartment. It was on the fourth floor of a building on a street just south-west of the Eiffel Tower. It was a narrow street, with apartment buildings on one side and an office block on the other. There wasn't much of a view. I had hoped to be able to see the river and the tower, but I could see neither.

The first few days were spent getting used to the area and sightseeing. To my surprise, I enjoyed being on my own, free to explore the city any way I wished. I went to the top of the Eiffel Tower twice. I strolled along the banks of the Seine, called in at the Louvre and Notre Dame. I tried to see the Mona Lisa through the hordes of tourists surrounding her. I drank coffee and wine and ate French food. Everywhere I went, Jo came with me in the urn.

At the end of the first week I phoned Jess.

"Everything okay?"

"Yes, we're enjoying it. It's as beautiful as she always said it would be."

"Have you decided what to do with Mom yet?"

"No, I'm still showing her the city."

There was a pause.

"You are okay, aren't you?"

"What do you mean?"

"I'm worried about you."

"Yes, I'm fine. Everything is going to be okay."

There was a sigh of relief on the other end of the phone.

"Okay, that's good to know. I got a bit worried."

I gave her my love and hung up. I looked at the urn.

"Well, Jo, it looks like Jess is worried about us. She shouldn't be. It's all been decided. She'll mourn for a while, but it'll pass. Dan will look after her, our parents will too."

I'd made my decision about three weeks before Jo died. It was one of those decisions where there is no debate, no internal conflict. Jess was settled with Dan and the baby. She was happy. I hoped she would understand my choice. This new world, a world without Jo, was somewhere I didn't want to live. There was no emotion associated with my choice, to me it was as straightforward as deciding what to eat at a restaurant. I had decided that after I'd scattered Jo's ashes I would kill myself.

The days passed and I finally made my decision about where Jo's ashes would be scattered. Into the Seine.

She would drift slowly down the river, eventually emerging into the English Channel. At that point, the world would be her oyster and she could end up anywhere. It was perfect. And then, after I had said goodbye, I would kill myself.

155

I decided that evening would be the best time. I made an occasion of it. I ate in a fancy restaurant. I walked along the bank of the river before crossing the bridge. I stopped halfway across. Looking down towards the dark water, I took my backpack off and removed the urn.

"Well, Jo, this is it. This is where we part. You always wanted to come to Paris, I hope you saw enough of the city. Now the world will be yours."

I sensed someone standing beside me. A familiar voice spoke.

"I did. Thank you."

I could smell her scent. I didn't dare look in the direction of her voice, instead I stared at the water below, the urn still clutched in my hand.

"It was always Paris for me. Ever since I was a child. I so wanted to see it. And you brought me, thank you."

I nodded.

"But why do you plan to kill yourself?"

"I want us to be together. Always. I can't stand the thought of living alone."

"It doesn't work like that. If you died by your own hand, we wouldn't be together. I would never see you again."

I hadn't thought of that.

"But what do I do?"

"You live. For yourself, for Jess, Dan and Amy. For me."

"It's too hard."

I sensed anger in the figure beside me.

"You're lucky. You get to live for another forty years. You get to see your daughter live her life.

You get to see Amy and your other, unborn, grandchildren grow up. You get to see the world. I don't. I have been denied all those things."

"You don't get to see us anymore?"

"After tonight, no."

There was no further explanation.

"What is it like?"

"What?"

"Death. Where you are now."

"Death is meaningless. Only life matters. And right now, I'm in Paris with my fool of a husband who has decided to kill himself in a fit of selfish pique."

I felt my face flushing red.

"David, if you kill yourself I will never forgive you."

She had always used those words when she was royally pissed at me. I had no option.

"Okay Jo. I won't."

"Promise?"

"Promise."

"Good. Now you can do what you came here for. Scatter my ashes. Then go to the apartment, pack and go home. Our family needs you."

I felt her move away from my side. I was alone again. I opened the urn and threw her ashes into the wind, watching as they settled onto the water below. I bid my wife farewell.

Before I left for the airport I phoned Jess.

"I'm so glad you're coming home. You sound

better than you did before. I was… worried about you. I thought you might do something stupid. I know you've been thinking about it. I could see it in your eyes."

I was horrified that Jess had guessed. It must have been such a burden on her.

"I was for a while, but not anymore."

"I'm happy to hear that."

"Jess, something happened tonight on that bridge. I think your mom visited me, spoke to me one last time. I know it sounds crazy, but I swear it's true."

"Mom was probably worried about you too."

"Maybe, or maybe I'm just going crazy."

My daughter, the pragmatic, practical girl, who was never scared of ghost stories when she was young, laughed gently.

'No, Dad, she came back to persuade you to keep living. I'm glad she did. Now you can be my dad and a grandfather again. Make up for us not having her around."

"I will Jess. One thing your mom showed me is that life is for living. I intend to do just that."

I hung up. I walked to the window of the apartment and sniffed the night air. It was fragrant and warm. The taxi I had called sounded its horn from the street below. I headed out. As I stood on the sidewalk I whispered to myself.

"Jo, it will always be Paris."

R. J. Meldrum is an author and academic. Born in

Scotland, he moved to Ontario, Canada in 2010 with his wife Sally. His interest in the supernatural is a lifetime obsession and when he isn't writing ghost stories, he's busy scouring the shelves of antique booksellers to increase his collection of rare and vintage supernatural books. During the winter months, he trains and races his own team of sled dogs.

He has had stories published by Sirens Call Publications, Horrified Press, Trembling with Fear, Darkhouse Books, Digital Fiction and James Ward Kirk Fiction.

THE HIT

Michael Penncavage

THE PHONE RANG, AND right away I knew that it was a job. It had been raining furiously since early afternoon and for some reason I always got the call for a job while it rained.

Of course it was Tony. For one guy, he seemed to need an awful lot of people dead.

"How have you been, Doris?" he asked, with a more-than-normal rasp in his voice. The cigars were doing him in.

"Just dandy. Who do you have for me?"

Silence on the other end. Tony was from the old school way of thinking. Only boys could be crooks. Only boys could be hitmen. He hated the fact that a long-haired blonde with 36-24-36 measurements not only did what I did, but did it better than anyone else he knew.

"My bookkeeper. Frank Lazimski. He's skimming off the ledgers. He thought that I was too stupid to find out."

I reached for the pack of Slims that lay on the couch. "How?"

"I want this one to be special."

"You want them *all* to be special."

"He thinks I am rewarding him for doing a good job."

From the tone in his voice I knew where this was heading. "You want me to take him out on a date?"

Silence again on the other end. I picked up my lighter off the coffee table.

"Just dinner. I made reservations at Ferraro's. Have him take you back to his place. Let him think he's getting lucky. Then take care of it."

I lit my cigarette. "When?"

"Tomorrow night. The car will pick you up at 7:45. The reservation's at 8 PM."

I glanced over at the calendar I had gotten from St. Luke's. October had a picture of Saint Christopher. "Tomorrow's Halloween."

"Trick-or-treat," he answered. The line went dead.

◆◆◆

Twenty-four hours didn't give me much time.

It was still overcast when I got up early the next morning. I looked up Frank's address in the phone book. Though he lived in a neighborhood I recognized, I still spent some of the morning driving around his house to get a feel for the streets.

I arrived home around midday. From the cedar

161

closet, I pulled out my black dress. It showed a lot of leg but made wearing the .45 impossible. From my dresser I took out a silver brooch that had been my mother's before she passed on. *It will help you meet a nice man when you go out on dates.*

◆◆◆

The car honked at exactly a quarter of. It was drizzling again, so I grabbed an umbrella as I ran out of the house.

I arrived at the restaurant and the maitre d' directed me to the table. My man was already there.

He was a short and skinny fellow with thick glasses, receding hairline, and bow tie. The orange candle on the table made his face reflect a strange glow. He looked exactly how I pictured a bookkeeper to be.

The conversation was light. Thinking I was nothing more than a call girl, he kept it simple.

The meal was good—though horribly overpriced. I paid, explaining to him again that Tony was *extremely* appreciative of him for doing such a good job.

Even through the thick glasses I could see the glint in his eye. I was all but assured of an invite to his house.

◆◆◆

We got into the car. I recognized Tony's personal driver, Sam, behind the wheel. He gave me a quick nod confirming he knew what was going down.

A half-hour later we pulled up to Frank's house.

As expected, he asked me in. I told Sam not to hang around. What that actually meant was—*park down the street a bit and wait.*

◆◆◆

Frank went to the bathroom to dandy himself up. I went over to the small bar to fix myself a gin and tonic. As I made the drink, a thick slice of moonbeam passed through the curtain and onto me. The clouds had passed and the moon was fully out—shining brilliantly. It was about time. *Enough of the rain.* Hopefully tomorrow would be a warm enough day that I could get some time in at the park.

Taking a generous sip from the glass, I looked down the hallway. Frank was still in the bathroom. Poor boy was either nervous or constipated.

I heard something shatter and break from within the bathroom.

"Everything all right in there, hon?"

No answer.

I removed the pistol from my purse and screwed the silencer on. After making sure there was a bullet in the chamber, I flicked the safety off. Sitting down on the sofa, I placed the pistol alongside a pillow. Though the moon was doing a good job of lighting up the room, there were plenty of shadows to conceal the gun.

The bathroom door opened and Frank finally came out.

At least I assumed it to be Frank, although the figure in the hall was in complete contrast to the wiry man who had gone into the bathroom. Though the shadows were keeping many of his features hidden, Frank's head was almost brushing against the ceiling.

A musty, foul scent trickled into the room. The first thing that crossed my mind was that someone forgot to do a courtesy flush.

Frank stepped into the room wearing a large, furry Halloween costume. Long pointy ears brushed up against the ceiling and a nasty set of molars protruded from his mouth. He looked like some kind of mutant wolf.

"I know it's Halloween but it's a little late to go to a costume party." I tried to act sincere. "You should have told me earlier. I could have arranged something…"

Raising his head up, he let out an ear-piercing howl. I watched as he turned to me and opened his jowls, revealing the biggest damned set of fangs I ever saw.

Grabbing a nearby La-Z-Boy chair with one of his paws, he flung it against a nearby wall as if he were tossing a bad book aside.

Problem, I thought. *Big Problem.*

I grabbed the gun, leveled it at him, and squeezed off two bullets. They struck him in the chest but he looked unfazed.

I raised my gun and placed a lead sinker into one of his eyes. Frank's head snapped back as if he had taken a punch in the nose, but still he didn't go down.

Thinking that the silencer was lessening the bullet's impact, I spun it off. Frank, however was amazingly quick. Before I could bring the gun back up, he bounded over the coffee table and was on me.

Boy did he stink.

He threw me into the same wall where he had sent the La-Z-Boy. I hit hard and the gun was jarred from my hand.

Before I could recover, Frank was on me again. His claws were like razors and they sunk deep into my shoulder as he grabbed me.

I cried out in pain as he pulled me up like a ragdoll. I tried breaking free but his grip was like a vice. Looking at the teeth that protruded from his mouth, I knew that I was goner if I didn't do something fast.

A flash caught my eye. *The brooch*. Without thinking, I pulled it from my dress and rammed it straight into the eye where I had shot a sinker. The pin sunk deep into the socket. Frank started howling as he lost his grip on me. I watched as he stumbled backward, clutching at his eye as he tried to remove the brooch. I really must have got him good for Frank only took a few more steps before he collapsed onto the coffee table.

I dropped to my knees and felt around and located my gun.

I approached the body cautiously. Frank was not moving. I watched in disbelief as the hair on what I thought was his costume began to retract. His snout and ears began to shrink as well. Even his physical size diminished before my eyes. It only took a minute before I was staring again at Frank the bookkeeper.

The brooch made a slurping sound as I yanked it out of his eye.

Putting the gun and brooch into my purse, I opened the front door and carefully looked outside. The neighbor's lights were off.

Lighting up a Slim, I tossed the match onto the rug. Taking a deep drag, I flicked the cigarette onto it as well. Five minutes and the whole place would be in flames.

I gently closed the door behind me. My shoulders throbbed as I walked to the limousine. I felt dizzy and nauseous. Sweat was beginning to bead on my brow. Frank had really cut me good with those fingernails. I hoped I didn't have an infection, or worse, rabies.

First thing in the morning, I was going to have it looked at.

This was going to cost Tony extra.

Michael Penncavage's story "The Cost of Doing Business" originally appeared in Thuglit, won the Derringer Award for best mystery. One of his stories, "The Converts" was recently filmed as a short movie, while another "The Landlord" was adapted as a play.

Fiction of his can be found in over 95 magazines and anthologies from 7 different countries such as Alfred Hitchcock Mystery Magazine (USA), Here and Now (England), Tenebres (France), Crime

Factory (Australia), Reaktor (Estonia), Speculative Mystery (South Africa), and Visionarium (Austria).
He has been an Associate Editor for Space and Time Magazine as well as the Editor of the horror/suspense anthology, Tales From a Darker State.

GIMLET

Gina Burgess

KATE STOOD IN FRONT OF a rusty gate, staring into the darkness. There was little to see except the vague shape of abandoned buildings. No people. No sign of the witch she'd organised to meet. Worry bubbled, brewing. She wasn't afraid waiting alone in the dark. The night wasn't scary, not compared to some things.

Against her will, her gaze drifted to the building behind the gate. The old school dorm stood out clearer than the rest of the forgotten complex. The sandstone surfaced from the night like a ghost.

Ghost.

Her nerves tightened, and she trembled.

Behind her, someone sniggered. Kate whirled around to find a teenage girl standing uncomfortably close. The girl switched on a torch, illuminating her black hair, kohl-ringed eyes and pale face.

"You scared me," Kate gasped.

The girl shrugged. "I'm not surprised. You look like you scare easily."

Kate's unease transformed into annoyance, but she pressed her lips together, determined to stay polite. This was surely who she'd been waiting for. Black dress. Striped stockings.

"You're the witch?"

The girl lifted an eyebrow. "I'm a medium. I need no wand or spell book to connect the dead and the living." She flicked her sleek hair. "I'm Gimlet, Penetrator of Realms."

"Seriously?"

Gimlet's cliché outfit and arrogance made Kate suspicious of a prank, but she needed help too badly to walk away.

She cleared her throat. "I mean, you're the perfect person to help me."

"I know, right? So, what do you need? No, let me guess. You want to connect with a boyfriend?"

"Something like that." A handsome, smiling face filled Kate's mind and her gut squeezed like a fist. With tears threatening to spill, she shoved thoughts of Adam away. "Will you help me?"

"I'm here, aren't I?" Gimlet shone her light on the dorm. "That's where it happened?"

Kate shivered. "Yeah."

For years Kate and her friends had snuck into the old boarding school to roam courtyards and classrooms, but they usually avoided the accommodation. Everyone believed it was haunted. Kate knew they were right.

"Should we head in?" Kate asked.

Gimlet looked Kate up and down. "You brave enough?"

"I've been inside plenty of times." Obsession, not bravery had drawn Kate inside. Occasionally it felt like an ordinary building. Other times she sensed a presence. Adam was there, somewhere, just out of reach.

And sometimes she really wasn't alone. Last visit, she'd stumbled across a girl hiding out in a bedroom. The meeting shattered them both, each shedding shudders and sobs. Kate hoped they didn't meet anyone this time, other than Adam.

Kate creaked the gate open and led the way to the dorm.

Inside was a foyer. The floor had probably been glossy white once, the walls sophisticated mauve. Neglect had turned everything murky, and plaster chunks hung from the sagging ceiling.

"I'll admit, I've never been in here," Gimlet said. "I thought the ghost stories were rubbish." Her gaze lingered on Kate. "Guess I was wrong." The torch lit stairs on either side of the foyer. "Where to?"

Kate frowned.

The kohl enhanced Gimlet's eyeroll. "We must go to the spot where it happened. It's the only way to connect with your boyfriend."

Of course. What better place to bridge the realms than the place where life had become death?

Gimlet gripped Kate's shoulder. "Don't be scared. I'll protect you."

She seemed so confident, but Kate still hadn't

decided if Gimlet was for real or full of crap. But since there was no better option...

"That way," Kate said, pointing.

They crossed the filthy floor and headed upstairs.

Their footsteps pattered in the narrow stairwell, then clonked, ringing out in the wide, wooden hallway. As they walked, Gimlet flicked the torch left and right, lighting rows of doors. Some stood open, revealing bed frames and yellowed lightshades over globes that hadn't shone in decades. Throughout the hallway lay other items. Mouldy dolls, a bike, even a fairy dress with a tiara and a bulky, metal, star-tipped wand.

Gimlet smirked. "Since you thought I was a witch..." She hefted the wand, and stuffed the heavy item in her belt. Her gaze rose to Christmas decorations drooping from the walls, more dust and spider web than tinsel.

"The girls went home for Christmas," Kate explained, recalling what she'd discovered in books. "Then the school shut down. The students weren't allowed back for their things."

Gimlet scanned the belongings, the items looters must have deemed too worthless to steal. "The girls lived most of their lives here, then overnight lost everything?"

Kate swallowed sorrow. "Many people have been robbed here, of so many things, in so many ways." Adam crept into her mind. She didn't sense him yet, but that didn't mean he wasn't there. "Can you feel anything, Gimlet? A presence?"

"The whole place reeks of misery but..."

171

Gimlet quietly chuckled. "It was a school once."

They reached a T in the hallway and Gimlet shone her torch to the side. "It's down this way, right?"

"How did you know?" Kate asked.

Gimlet formed a strange, sad smile. "Sometimes, I just know." She led the way, weaving through another cluttered corridor, passing room after room.

At the end of the hall, she stopped and faced a door. "In here?"

"Yes." How could Gimlet know? Had Kate dragged her feet, giving away her reluctance, or could Gimlet be a true medium?

As the door swung open, Kate's heart galloped. Not once in all her visits had she found the strength to step into the room where it happened. She whimpered as the torch lit up a row of grimy showers and baths.

Gimlet took her hand. "It's okay. I'm with you."

She swayed the light back and forth, eventually stilling it on shiny, white porcelain. The clean bath had no place in the ruins.

"I see," Gimlet murmured. "The bath is clean now, but I can sense the past. Not long ago it glistened red." She shuddered. "So much blood."

So much blood and pain and horror.

"Murder," Gimlet said.

Despite her fear, Kate breathed out a relieved sigh. She had no doubt now; Gimlet was a real medium and she could find Adam.

"Time to connect to your lover," Gimlet said.

"You ready?"

Kate trembled but she managed a nod.

Gimlet grinned. "Time to watch a master at work."

She punched the air. Once, twice, three times. The first movement did little, creating a vague breeze, but the second sent vibrations through the air. The third strike made the room shimmer and Adam appeared near the bath.

Kate hadn't expected the worlds to connect so easily, or to find Adam so quickly. Surprise made her gasp.

Pressing a hand over her mouth, Gimlet dragged her into the corridor. "Nothing's dividing our realms anymore," she hissed. "Some people don't handle these meetings well, so before going back in, be certain you want to do this."

Did she? She was no longer sure. Sucking back shock, she peeked inside. Adam's back was to her as he bent over the bath. She couldn't see his handsome face, but he was even more muscular than she remembered.

Gimlet nudged her. "You going to speak to him?"

Kate trembled and swallowed but she couldn't form words.

Gimlet frowned. "Isn't that why we're here? For one last 'I love you'?"

Kate choked on a sob and shook her head.

"Then why?" Gimlet's gaze flicked from Kate, to Adam and back again, then slowly her mouth widened. "He's not an old boyfriend, is he?"

Before Kate could reply, Adam grew still, then

shot to his feet. With a torch in one hand and a knife in the other, he whirled, scanning the room. It seemed he could sense their presence but he'd yet to spot them.

Gimlet's eyes widened, and she pointed past Adam, to the bath. A girl lay limply within it. Kate didn't share Gimlet's surprise. She'd expected Adam to bring a girl. It was why she'd needed to connect their worlds. There could be no more girls. No more victims.

"No more murders!" Kate shouted and charged into the room.

Seeing her, Adam hollered and stumbled away, and Kate raced for the bath. She braced herself for blood and death, but the bath was clean. Adam had parted the unconscious girl's clothes, baring her skin but he hadn't yet cut her. Of course not. He liked his victims awake. He enjoyed seeing their terror as he killed them.

On their first date, Kate had expected the movies or a restaurant. Instead Adam had brought her to the haunted dorm and made her one of the ghosts. And he continued to kill innocent girls. Often, Kate found them stumbling about the building, too shocked to realise they'd died.

"No more!"

Fear gone, lost beneath fury, Kate dived at her killer. She thrust fists at his chest, but there was no connection. Momentum sent her staggering into him, then through him, and she met the solid wall. "No!" She spun to face Gimlet. "You said the worlds were connected. There was nothing separating us."

"You can see and hear the world of the living," Gimlet said, "but you can't touch it. You're a ghost made of ether, not flesh. A spirit, not a superhero."

Horror threatened to floor Kate, and she wailed. All the watching, waiting, planning, hoping—all for nothing. She could scream and rant, but it wouldn't stop Adam's knife swinging.

Adam apparently realised she couldn't touch him, because he laughed, then stepped forward to leer over Kate.

"You're no match for me, Kate. No stronger than you were in life." He smirked. "You were so easily fooled, so desperate to be my girlfriend. You didn't even question why I brought you here. None of you ever do."

He waved his knife under Kate's nose. She tried not to flinch, but her body betrayed her. Laughing, he turned to the sleeping girl.

"Don't," Kate croaked. "Let her live. Please."

Her words were pointless. No amount of begging had helped on the night he ended her life, and it wouldn't help Adam's latest victim either. Kate sobbed.

Gimlet stepped into the room. "Hey, Adam."

Adam ignored her, patting the sleeping girl's cheek, coaxing her to wake.

Gimlet approached the bath. "Kate's no superhero. She can't touch the living. But me..." She tilted her head, cracking her neck, then grinned. "I'm the real deal."

She lifted her arm and silver flashed in her hand. A knife? No. The fairy wand. With teeth clenched, she swung. Adam raised his hands, but he was too slow. The wand struck his face, a star point slicing his cheek. A second blow knocked him to the floor and a third knocked his lights out.

♦♦♦

Kate and Gimlet watched from across the street as medics helped the dazed girl into the ambulance and police shoved Adam into a cop car. Gimlet could have killed Adam, but she and Kate decided they didn't want trash like him in their afterlife.

"That was fun." Gimlet twirled the bloodstained wand. "I think I'll keep this. Seems a wand can be handy sometimes."

"Thanks for the help," Kate said. The words seemed too small, a poor fit for the huge favour.

"No biggie," Gimlet said. "Easy work for the Penetrator of Realms." She grinned and backed away, heading for the shadows she'd arrived in. "Being a superhero tonight was fun. I could get used to it."

"Really?" Kate said. "Well, there's a rumour little kid ghosts have been turning up in suspicious numbers. It could be the work of a serial killer."

"That so?" Gimlet asked. "Cool, I'll check it out." She stepped deeper into the shadows, then stopped and faced Kate. "Want to help?"

Help save lives? Fight killers? It wasn't what Kate had planned for her life, not even close, but she wasn't alive anymore. Grinning, she dashed to Gimlet's side and together they entered the shadows.

Gina Burgess is a writer from Tasmania. Her stories range from unsettling to uplifting and often take readers down unexpected paths. Her fiction has appeared in "Wizards in Space," "Mystery Weekly Magazine" and "Re:Fiction." When not writing, Gina creates art, runs long distances, and travels across Australia in pursuit of her favourite bands.

BONUS MATERIAL

The first anthology in the Read on the Run Series is *A Step Outside of Normal*.   As a bonus, we have included two stories from that anthology, that fit in well with the theme of this anthology.

RAGE

Catherine Valenti

IT WAS SUPPOSED TO BE a nice four-mile hike in the forest. Our little walk by the river. A single track trail with the sweet aroma of pine trees and fresh air surrounding us. We'd hiked this path many times.

I used to enjoy this walk. Now, my chest was tight and my steps were as measured as the words that came out of my mouth. I paid little attention to the chirping of the birds, the splash of the river, and the pungent smell of pine needles. Because it had gone too smoothly today with Eddie. I had really missed the signals this time. I hadn't realized this was one of Eddie's "bad days", or I would have feigned being sick. Of course he would have pounded me anyway, but at least it would have been at our apartment. Where I could at least find some solace in a corner. Not stuck in the middle of nowhere.

We had only gone about a mile when he started in on me. "You're a lazy bitch. I come home, wanting to take you for a nice hike, and the place is a pigsty. A pigsty."

He grabbed my arm, digging in deep and tight.

"Eddie, please," I said, and tried to quiet my gasp. It would make things worse to argue. I wished to be anywhere else but here. With him. I hated myself for being so weak. So scared. So helpless.

"Tell me something, Cassie," he growled, his soulless gaze inches from my face. His spittle hit my cheeks. I scrunched my eyes tight and pulled back as far as I dared. I didn't want to see those icy, vicious eyes, bloodshot with fury. "Don't I give you everything you want? Everything you need? What do you do all day? Meet some guy at the bar?"

I didn't answer, didn't try to tell him I was at work all day. Every day. It didn't matter. He was going to hit me. I felt it before his fist reached my face. When I stumbled he didn't try to catch me, and I landed in the middle of sharp branches and rocks.

He yanked me to my feet. Spewed profanities at me. Hit me again. I screamed, and begged him to stop. I told him I was sorry, it wouldn't happen again. Pleaded with him to take me home.

Eddie punched me again, right under my ribs. When the force spun me around I felt a sharp blow to my back. I couldn't breathe, couldn't talk. I lay on the ground, curled up and rocking back and forth.

When I could finally catch my breath, I stared right into his eyes and screamed. I didn't care. He couldn't cause me more pain than I had endured already. "No more, Eddie. I'm not taking this anymore."

He backed away. I had caught him off-guard. I choked back a sob.

"What the hell did you say to me?" He raised both hands, clenched into fists. "You worthless piece of crap."

Something snapped inside, and for the first time in my life I didn't care about the consequences. I managed to stand as Eddie watched—that ugly sneer on his face. With speed fueled by fury I ran at him, and when I hit him we both tumbled down. He jumped to his feet before I could get off my knees, grabbed me and flung me over his shoulder. Eddie was a big man, muscular and solid. I was short, thin, and no match for him. I tried to wriggle out of his grasp, but he held on tightly as he marched down the path. After about twenty paces he took a sharp right. I couldn't see where we were going but I could hear the river roar below.

I screamed once more—when he lifted me off his shoulders and threw me down into the river. I hit the rocks, and felt sharp pains joining the dull ones he had inflicted earlier. I gasped for breath, trying to keep my head above water. It was impossible. The river was moving too fast and it was ice-cold. Each time my head bobbed out of the water, I set my sights on the shore, but it was so far away. I smashed into another rock.

Keep fighting, Cassie. Don't let him win. I swung my arms, kicked my legs. *He will pay for this.* My world faded away into nothing.

◆◆◆

I wasn't sure how much time had passed, but it couldn't have been more than a half hour. I was still soaking wet, and sprawled out in a few inches of water, only a few feet from the river. Gone were the boulders and rapids, the river had widened and the water flowed gently past me. I dragged myself to a small patch of grass, ignoring the shrubs that caught on my clothes. My whole body must have gone into shock, I had trouble feeling much of anything.

"I will never, ever be with that man again." I stood, wavering unsteadily with the sun beating down. "He was trying to kill me." I faced the water and watched the gentle splash of the river against the smaller rocks that poked through by the shoreline. It had been a long time since I had allowed myself to get angry, but now my entire body raged with fury.

The only way I could be certain of freedom from Eddie and the physical and emotional pain he caused me was to get rid of him. I had tried to hide from him before, several times, until I realized that his punishment once he found me was almost unbearable. And never worth it.

I would have to kill him. I didn't know how, but I would have to do it.

Exhaustion hit me hard, and I collapsed on a patch of grass. My eyes closed and a soothing, peaceful wave flowed through me. I needed to rest and clear my mind.

My eyes squinted open when bright rays of the setting sun hit my face. A surge of power and clarity shot through my body. I felt an inner strength I never realized I could muster. His murder attempt was the last straw.

How odd. I ran my gaze over my battered and bruised body. *I'm not even scared anymore, I'm just furious.*

There was a little path by the shore, and I staggered toward it. I hoped it would lead me to safety, but inside I wondered if it would instead lead me into the greatest danger I had ever faced.

The path grew wider and smoother. I didn't have to worry about tripping or losing my way, and I had plenty of time to ponder my next move. I needed to get inside the apartment without being seen, and somehow figure out how I was going to handle Eddie. My soon to be very-ex-boyfriend.

"But y-you're dead!" His shaky voice complemented his wide eyes and open mouth.

I smiled. It was a good feeling to catch him off guard. My plan, the one I hatched while I was making my way back home, was going swimmingly. *Oh, that's clever Cassie. Swimmingly!*

"I've never felt better, *dear*. The news of my

183

demise was a bit premature."

My plan didn't include exactly how to get Eddie out of the apartment, and now that I was face-to-face with him I had more thinking to do. Whatever I decided to do, I would have to be quiet. I had tried to slip in unnoticed, but there was always a chance one of the neighbors had seen me. Then there were those pesky security cameras.

As I contemplated these things, my hand holding the pistol dropped slightly. Eddie must have noticed, and he took two big steps toward me. I had no more time to think. He was coming for me.

I threw the gun at him as hard as I could. A risky move. I could have missed, and he might have picked it up and used it on me. As luck would have it my instinct was right on.

The butt of the Glock cracked him on the left temple of his head, and it bounced off him right back to me. Eddie collapsed in a heap. I picked up my weapon and walked over to assess the damage.

A small cut on his head, but he was out cold. What a lucky shot, because I sure as hell couldn't aim that well. The gods were on my side tonight.

Of course, that left the dilemma of how to get him out of our apartment and into his car without being seen. I closed my eyes and did my best to relax. Since I'd been with Eddie, I don't think I'd felt calm for more than an hour at a time. A little peace would be nice.

As soon as I felt myself slipping into a twilight sleep, my brain jerked me back to reality with a little reminder. *He's not tied up. If he wakes up and you are dead asleep, then you'll be just plain dead.*

I glanced down at my former Prince Charming. Eddie, the would-be-killer, out cold. I wanted to kick him in the face, but bad temper on my part was bound to end in tragedy. My own tragedy. I didn't know how, but I felt deep inside me that unless I took the straight and narrow path to revenge, it could all backfire.

"I've been through too much to let you win by default," I muttered as I pulled my foot away from his face and turned to his desk to locate something to bind him with. Several rolls of tape were neatly stacked in the forward tray, with a pair of scissors next to them. For once I was thankful he was obsessed with perfect order. I grabbed the black electrician's tape. This might work.

First I wrapped a two foot length of tape around his right wrist, and pulled it around his back, then I brought his left wrist over and taped the two together.

I worked fast, securing his wrists and ankles with most of the tape in the drawer. When I stepped back to survey my handiwork, I admit I was quite pleased with my efforts. It wasn't pretty. I would never win a prize for neatness with this mess. What I lacked in presentation, however, I made up for in effectiveness. It would be a challenge for anyone, even with the sharpest of knives, to cut through the layers of assorted tape binding this monster.

I took one last piece of clear plastic postal tape and placed it over his mouth. It would be especially satisfying when I wanted him to talk. I would pull that piece off, hoping that it would yank out every bit of the scruffy beard he kept because he thought it made him look sexy.

Eddie started stirring, whimpering and moving his head. I debated about another smack to the head, but decided to show some charity. For now.

I left him on the floor by the sofa and went into our bedroom, shutting the door behind me. I needed to calm down, away from Eddie's frustrated moans, and think about my next step. I glanced around the room—to the bed made to military preciseness. His dresser, with his keys arranged in the tray, his car key fob pointing precisely toward the door, as always.

Here's where I fell in love with that scoundrel. Here's where he touched me in places that sent me to heaven. Here's where he gave me my first black eye, and my first broken rib, and somehow talked me into believing it was my own fault.

This was not putting me in a meditative mood, and I felt I needed to be there in order to figure out how I could get Eddie out of his apartment, into his car, and... well, wherever I decided we should go.

About a half hour later I opened my eyes and knew what I needed to do and how to accomplish it. Once the steps were clear, the actual implementation would be easy. Almost too easy, I thought. Eddie was awake, but groggy, and silent as I dragged him to his car. He probably didn't want another crack on the head.

◆◆◆

It was almost dark as I drove down the highway, then later the two-lane country road, and much later the bouncy gravel and dirt jeep trail that led to some obscure camping spots. I kept up conversational chatter with my ex-boyfriend.

"Eddie, I know you're wondering what I'm doing. What will happen to you." I tried to keep the excitement out of my voice. "Well, aren't you?"

I heard a low "mmmhmm" and some frantic noises from the back seat, where I had thoughtfully seat-belted him in.

"If you're asking me to let you go, well, you know I can't," I said. "If I released you, I could only imagine two outcomes. One, you go to the cops and cause trouble for me. Or two, you come after me and I end up dead. Really dead this time." I snuck a peek to the back, seeing only his shadowed figure in the dark. "I doubt you'd make the same mistake twice."

From the squeals, groans, and other assorted noises he emitted, I was certain he was trying to assure me that he would never come near me again, and would never talk to the cops.

Like I believed him after the three years we spent together.

I felt a kick against my seat back. His legs were bound together, he could go nowhere without me, yet still he was trying to hurt me.

My body shook with sudden fury. "Stop it!" I screamed. Immediate silence. "Full of lies! You are so full of lies, full of crap. I spent years trying to believe you, then covering for you. I lied to my friends, my family, my coworkers."

My anger was so strong it threatened to turn to tears. I took several deep breaths.

187

"No one knew. Maybe they suspected, but I was so good at lying about you, that no one ever, ever asked me." I shook my head. "They never asked—Cassie, how did you get that bruise on your arm? Or—Cassie, are you sure it's allergies? It looks like you've been crying."

Eddie was smart enough to stay quiet.

"I loved you, Eddie!" I couldn't help it, tears ran down my face. Dammit, I think I still loved him. And hated him. "I did everything for you. I tried so hard to be the person you claimed you wanted, but nothing was ever good enough."

There was a giant pothole ahead. I sped up, aimed right for it, braced myself, and smiled when we bounced hard over it. Eddie's precious little car with its fancy wheels and perfect pearl-black paint job jolted and shuddered. Maybe his head had slammed against the window when we hit. I could only hope.

I wasn't done with Eddie. Not yet, not for quite awhile. "Then, when I thought you were taking me on a lovely walk in the woods, a nice romantic time spent in nature—when I thought that maybe you had changed and things would be different..." I couldn't help it, the sobs started coming and I was gasping for breath.

"You hit me in the face... Then you punched me in my side, under my ribs. Where you knew it would hurt the most." I paused, trying to stop the tears. "When I turned to run away, you slammed your fist in my back. That wasn't good enough, was it?" I took another look in the rearview mirror. Eddie sat still as a stone. "You picked me up and threw me into the river. Like a piece of trash."

The turnoff was just ahead. I pulled in, and the little sports car bounced and strained on the rutted dirt road. Stout branches scraped against the top and sides, screeching like fingernails on a chalkboard. His car, his pride and joy, was not built for rutted roads. *Too bad, Eddie.*

Finally I stopped. When I opened the car door I could hear the rushing of the river in the distance. Eddie would meet the same fate he tried to give me. That would be karma.

"Funny," I said, not really to Eddie. More to myself. "I thought being this close to the water, especially with you along, would make me nervous. But actually..." I opened the door and looked straight at Eddie. "Really, I'm okay. I feel good. I feel great. Better than I've been in a very long time."

And I did feel fine. I had waited years to be free of the toxic, painful hold he had on me. That entire time, everything I did felt fake. My smiles never formed on the inside, bursting out to the world, like they were doing right now.

I unbuckled this pathetic bundle of crap, and pulled him out. He stumbled and did a perfect face-plant. I guess I forgot that his ankles were still bound together. Oh well.

This was a beautiful spot. Perfect for what I had in mind. We were in the midst of a small clearing, with two spaces for campsites. It was remote enough with no facilities and I was certain we wouldn't be interrupted. The headlights shown on a fire pit with open space around it. Large pines

189

towered over and around us, creating a safe, secure, private haven. When I looked up at the stars, the moon peered over the top of one of the trees, brightening the area. Almost a full moon.

I closed my eyes and felt as though I were up there, among the moon and the stars, looking down at this wondrous clearing. I took a deep breath, and the smells of pine, and flowers, and water, and clean, crisp air nearly made me cry. It was so lovely.

But I had work to do, and the spell was broken as I opened my eyes.

"I could stay here forever," I said to Eddie. He was curled up in a fetal position. I leaned in close to him, and grabbed one end of the tape over his mouth. I pulled, not slowly and carefully but with short little jerks that made him cringe and whine.

He had tears in his eyes, from pain, or maybe fear. I looked closer, right into those deep brown eyes of his. It wasn't fear. It wasn't pain. Eddie was enraged.

Once he could speak he literally growled at me. "You are a dead woman, Cassie." His voice rasped and broke, and he coughed a few times. Must have been the dust and ashes his face had been buried in when he hit the ground. "I should have sliced you up when I had the chance. I will make you scream, and you will wish with every breath that I would kill you and put you out of your misery."

I should have been terrified. Every other time he spoke to me like that, even on the phone when we were miles apart, I had been paralyzed with fear, knowing the worst was going to happen very soon.

But now a strange, comforting sense of calm and peace drifted over me. His words didn't hurt, not anymore, and they certainly didn't scare me. His ankles and wrists were bound so securely there was no way he could escape.

"You couldn't kill me, Eddie," I said, as I sat back and watched him. Studied him. "You tried yesterday, and I climbed out of that river, over those rocks, and right back into your life. I'm stronger than you ever realized." I smiled, just a bit. "Stronger than *I* ever realized."

I stood up and grabbed the bag I had stowed in the front seat. There were matches inside. I could use those for a fire. The air swirling around was warm enough, but fires were part of camping.

Eddie began cursing at me, and continued for several minutes. I ignored him as I gathered up some twigs, pine needles, and leaves, and started a little fire. Once it had caught, I added a few large branches I found close by.

I turned my back on him, and watched the flames and sparks dance around the pit. The warm light drifted over me, washing me with peace from head to toe. "Eddie," I said. "You tried to kill me in the river, then again when you tried to get the pistol away from me. It didn't work. I'm not going to give you another chance to kill me. Ever."

The fire crackled and hissed. It was telling me secrets. "We have secrets too, dear." I bent down and looked him in the eye. "Dirty little secrets, Eddie."

"What the hell are you talking about? Get me the hell out of this tape." He glared at me. "I have to piss. If you at least untie my legs so I can walk, I might consider leaving you alive after this is over. Bitch."

"Really?" I shook my head. "I suggest you stop talking nonsense. I'll grab some blankets from the trunk of the car. Even with the fire going, you might be cold on the ground. Oh, and do you want a drink of water? Just trying to make you happy, *dear*."

He didn't respond. He probably was thirsty. I propped him up against a log and gave him several sips of bottled water until he shook his head and turned away. I covered him with one of the blankets. Damn, I was nice.

"You should try to sleep," I said. "We have an exciting day tomorrow. I won't spoil the surprise, you'll find out in the morning. It will be perfect, trust me."

I took two of the blankets over to the other side of the fire. Eddie kept watching me. I wasn't worried about him trying to do anything. The worst that could happen is he'd try to roll his body out of here, but he had several miles to travel before he would hit a road with any traffic on it.

Now that would be an entertaining sight to see.

I laid the first blanket on a cleared patch of ground, then settled in and covered myself with the second one, snuggling in. With the heat from the crackling fire, I wasn't cold, but the blankets were comforting. Odd, but for the first time since I'd met Eddie, I knew I was safe.

I must have fallen asleep, because when I opened my eyes the dull gray of dawn coated everything. The sun was still hidden, probably by the tall trees. Not a cloud in the overhead sky.

Eddie had moved a few feet, more than likely to try to get comfortable, which wasn't going to happen. He was snoring fitfully.

"Good morning, sunshine," I said, and watched him until his eyes opened.

He let out a groan. "This is killing me, Cassie. You gotta get me out of here. I can't feel my feet."

"You won't need to feel your feet," I said, a little surprised he spewed no profanity, at least not yet. "How about a little swim?" He glared, but I saw fear behind his bravado. "Don't tell me you're surprised. It should have been clear last night, since we ended up right at the river's edge."

"You are crazy, bitch. You'll never get away with it." Eddie jerked his head toward his bound feet. "They'll find me with this tape crap all over and they'll know you did it."

"Hmm." I thought about what he said. "Maybe I should cut off the tape before I throw you in the water."

Eddie nodded.

"I'll think about it," I said as I walked over to him and grabbed his ankles. He screamed as I dragged him toward the water.

Ah, here came the profanities. I wished I could cover my ears, but my hands were otherwise occupied. "You're killing me, Cassie. That hurts like hell."

I ignored him. We had about thirty yards to the edge of the river, and I needed to save my strength. The traverse took awhile, and I had to jerk him over a few rocks and heavy brush. Even bundled up like he was with all that tape he was a handful to haul.

When we reached the edge of the boulders hanging over the rushing water, I looked down, and then at Eddie. "It's about a ten foot drop, Eddie dear," I said. My voice actually sounded cheerful. I was going to end a human life, and I wasn't even nervous. Or contrite. Maybe because he hadn't acted like a human in years. "If I remember correctly the area you dropped me into was twice as far down. There were rock and rapids. This looks fairly smooth."

He scowled at me, but there were beads of perspiration on his forehead, and he seemed to be trembling slightly.

"Don't you think you have an excellent chance of survival? No?"

"Hurry and do it then," he said, spitting the words out with venom. "Get me out of this tape and just do it."

I laughed. I couldn't help it. "Now what's the challenge in that?" I said, when I finally stopped to catch my breath.

Eddie looked at me, shock and fear in his eyes as I put my hands under his shoulder and back. I rolled him once.

"No!" he screamed. Finally he realized I had been serious. "Stop! I'll do anything you want! I'll confess to the cops, and leave you alone forever. Just stop. For God's sake, stop!"

"I don't feel like stopping, Eddie," I said as I gave him a final push that sent him over the edge.

His body did a barrel roll once before it hit the water. It splashed under and bobbed up several times as the current carried him away. Only once did I notice he was face up to the surface, then down he went again.

I watched him for as long as I could see him, waving slowly until he was out of sight.

As I drove his car back to the apartment I contemplated my next move. I knew his body would be found, and it was likely someone would find the campsite. It wasn't clear to me how I would establish an alibi, but somehow I thought no one would believe I could have overpowered him, trussed him up, and dragged him to the river. He was almost twice as big as me.

Fear and anger, and pure survival instincts had been the impetus. When he dumped me in the river, threw me away like yesterday's garbage and left me to die, something deep inside me had emerged. Where I had been weak around him, I was now strong. Fear morphed into anger. The moral code I lived by was shot to hell. I had purposely, gleefully, without a smidgen of remorse—taken a human life. Or, well—Eddie's life.

♦♦♦

Once I entered the apartment, I immediately threw my clothes and the blankets into the washing machine and flipped it on. Then I took a hot shower. It purified my soul, and the tenseness throughout my body melted away.

I wrapped myself in my warm, fuzzy robe and curled up on the sofa. A spark of agitation grew deep within me. I was missing something, a big something. I couldn't focus, so I turned on the television for some background noise. I needed to take my mind off the events of the morning.

The news at noon was on, and the male anchor had just finished a story about a fatal four-car crash on the interstate. He turned it back to co-anchor Colby Gray. She had blond hair that flipped up at her shoulders. That's all I noticed as the words on the blue screen behind her read "Drowning Victim Found."

I gasped. How could they have found Eddie so quickly? It had only been a few hours. My heart started pounding. What would I do, how would I explain all of this? I wouldn't have time to dry the blankets before the police came. The car was still covered with dust, and pine needles lodged in the windshield.

I grabbed the remote control and turned the volume up. I heard the words but they were slow to seep into my brain.

"...the body of twenty-six year old Cassie Munroe. Authorities are investigating the cause of death, as some injuries are of suspicious origins. She was reported missing yesterday around noon by her boyfriend, Edward Smith, who claimed they were hiking when she slipped and fell on some rocks into the river. At this time investigators consider Smith a person of interest."

I sat straight, and dropped the remote. I was Cassie Munroe. That was my photo on the news. That was my body, they said. But how...

I jumped as I heard loud pounding on the door. "Police, open up." Then the door blew in and three armed officers swarmed into the apartment. I plastered myself against the wall, hands over my head.

One of them brushed past me as if I wasn't there. They split up, quickly spreading out into the other rooms.

As they gathered back in the living room, the one that had pushed by me said, "The place is empty, Sergeant. Someone was just here though. There's water in the shower stall and the washer is running.

I squinted against a sudden bright light shining around me. Why would the cops be using a flashlight in the middle of the day?

I couldn't understand why they couldn't see me, until I realized that I was actually floating above them, close to the ceiling.

My face turned upward as confusion melted away. A wave of pure love and peace washed over me. It was time to leave.

By day, Cathy is a mild-mannered reporter for a national online news service for lawyers and news media. After hours, she is an editor, runs a small publishing company with her business partner, and writes paranormal and science fiction stories as well as motivational non-fiction.
She has a short story in "The Ancient," an anthology by authors known as the Seven, as well as stories in several of the Read on the Run

anthologies, and is currently working on a novel. Cathy lives in Idaho, where in addition to writing, she enjoys hiking, running, skiing, and dancing. Visit her website at https://catherinevalenti.com

HELL OF A DAY

Laurie Axinn Gienapp

THE GROUND TREMBLED and the smell of sulfur hung in the air over the valley like a blanket from hell. And things didn't look any better than they smelled. A sick day seemed like a good idea. Sadly, a sick day was not in the cards for me.

"Lou, are you going to stand there with the door open all day? You know I hate the smell of sulfur."

I sighed. "Yes, Ma, I know you hate the smell of sulfur, you take every opportunity to remind me." I closed the door and stood there for a moment with my head leaning against the jamb, before I turned and went back to the kitchen and my breakfast. My cereal had gone soggy of course, and after poking at it a few times with my spoon, I dumped it down the garbage disposal.

"Don't leave your dirty bowl in the sink, Lou. You know I hate dirty dishes in the sink."

"Yes, Ma. I know you hate dirty dishes in the sink." I rinsed my bowl and set it in the dish drainer.

"Are you going to work today?"

Again, I sighed. "Of course I'm going to work today. Monday through Friday, I always go to work."

This time she was the one who sighed. "I really wish you didn't work for that man."

I'd heard this before, of course, and I knew what came next. Long ago I'd lost count of how many times we'd had this same conversation.

"Can't you get a job with someone else?" she whined.

I didn't bother answering. After all, as I said I'd had this conversation many times before. We both knew each other's lines as well as we knew our own. I put on my jacket, grabbed my pack and headed out the door. Mom could finish our conversation on her own, without me.

I trudged down the road. I could never decide if it was a blessing or a curse that I lived so close to work. Sure, there was no traffic, but on the other hand I never felt like I truly escaped either work or home, because wherever I was, the other one was so close. Just one more bit of proof that my life was truly pathetic. I lived with my mother, I worked for my father, my parents had divorced before I was even born, and they hated each other's guts. But under the circumstances, how could you expect anything else?

I walked into the main office, nodding at the security guard as I walked by. I stamped my time card, returned it to its proper slot, and headed out to the yard in back.

"Morning, Lou."

"Morning, Dad."

"It's going to be a busy day, today."

"Yessir. I smelled the sulfur at the house."

He grimaced. "I wish you'd move over to the other side of town. I can't believe you still live with that woman."

I sighed. "Dad, we've been over this enough times. I'm not leaving Mom, she needs me."

He shook his head and headed for the control booth. As he walked away, he called over his shoulder, "Start with the southwest corner, today. That's where the worst of it is."

I moved over to the corner he'd indicated, slid my pack off my shoulder, and took out the vacu-collect. I started it up and began moving the nozzle in a wide sweeping pattern, suctioning up the scattered brimstone.

This was a pretty mindless task, and I'd done it often enough that I could practically have done this in my sleep. My mind wandered as I worked my way across the yard and my thoughts returned to my parents. It was actually more of a surprise that they ever got together, than that they'd split up. Mom's family was in charge of Hell's fires, and Dad's family was in charge of Hell's brimstone. I mean, come on, how could their relationship have been anything other than explosive?

Finally, the whistle blew, indicating the end of the day, and I turned off my vacu-collect with a sigh of relief. There had been more loose brimstone than usual, and it had been a tough shift. I waved goodbye to Dad and he called something out, but I was too far away to hear. So I gave him a big smile and waved again, and trudged home. As I approached the house, I saw that it was dark. Worried that something was wrong, I quickened my pace.

I opened the door, calling out "Ma?"as I stepped inside.

At first there was no answer, and I was about to call out again when I heard her reply from the other room. "Lou? I'll be right out, dear. I guess I lost track of time."

I reached over to turn on a lamp, but nothing happened when I pressed the switch.

"Oh, and there's a problem with the power, dear. I called the electric company but they said it won't be fixed until tomorrow."

Well that explained the dark house and the lamp switch. I shrugged out of my pack and my jacket, hung both of them on the hook by the door, and collapsed onto the couch.

"How was your day, dear?"

"Just a normal day, Ma. Gathering up the loose brimstone."

"Ugh. I hate the smell of sulfur."

"Yes, Ma, I know."

And then it hit me. What Dad was trying to tell me when I left, was that I had forgotten to empty and sanitize my vacu-collect. Which meant that the device was filled with brimstone dust and vapors. The device that was in my pack. The pack that was on the hook. And with a sense of foreboding, I knew what was going to happen next. I jumped up with the plan of moving my pack outside, but before I could reach it Mom walked into the living room, carrying a candle.

As the house exploded, I thought to myself, "Well, this has been a hell of a day."

Laurie Gienapp lives in northeastern Massachusetts with her husband and their two cats. She and her husband spend as much time as they can either ocean fishing or ballroom dancing. The cats spend as much time as they can, sleeping. Her sci-fi/adventure story "The Weatherman" was published in 2016, and she has had a number of short stories appear in Read on the Run anthologies, since then. Irregularly, Laurie posts to her blog at www.teapotmusings.blogspot.com

Visit her website at www.lauriegienapp.com

OTHER TITLES PUBLISHED BY SMOKING PEN PRESS

Links for digital and print versions of our titles are available from our website Smokingpenpress.com

Read on the Run is a series of anthologies with stories that are short enough to finish while you're going about your daily business, but long enough to tell a good tale.

A Step Outside of Normal

A Step Outside of Normal presents seven situations which are almost, but not quite, normal. Not really supernatural, not really fantasy, not really general fiction. Instead, they're each a little bit "off". And short, to suit your busy lifestyle.

Hell of a Day is about a young man who has to deal with divorced parents who don't like each other... but with an unusual setting. Sunnybrook Acres is a story of a retirement home, with an unexpected cadre of residents. Pirates looks at the world out of the eyes of a young child. Always is a tender story about loss, except that maybe it's not so tender. Xyxyx examines the beginning of the world, but perhaps not our world. The Double presents a young woman who appears to have a doppelganger. And Rage—well, you'll just have to read that one.

This is the first in the Read on the Run series of short

OTHER TITLES BY SMOKING PEN PRESS

story anthologies. Two of these stories - Hell of a Day, and Sunnybrook Acres, appear in Volume 2 of Vampires, Zombies and Ghosts, as bonus material.

"Good short entertainment." -- Amazon

"An excellent read for those who like stories with a twist." --Amazon

A Bit of a Twist

The twelve short stories presented in A Bit of A Twist are each mostly normal and ordinary, but somewhere in the story is a twist. In "David's Not Here", "Marriage Counselor", "Down Home", "River Road", "Happily Ever After", and "Blind Date", the ending takes a bit of a twist from what you were probably expecting. "The Chateau de Puyguilhem" and "The Wish" take stories you're already familiar with, and give the whole thing a bit of a twist. "Reunion", "Eternal Youth", and "Aliens Among Us" each have a bit of a mental twist. And "Air of Authority" shows what happens when you twist around words.

As you read these stories, you will also discover that many of them involve some degree of revenge. Because, after all, what is revenge but twisting someone's own actions back on them?

And as always, each story in the Read on the Run series of anthologies is short, to suit your busy lifestyle.

"Great short story collection." -- Amazon

Uncommon Pet Tales

Fifteen short stories involving pets.

But don't think for a moment that you'll "See Spot Run", or that Lassie will save her master who's fallen in the well. Those are common pet tales, and these are Uncommon Pet Tales.

Within this collection, you'll find a little bit of romance, a little bit of revenge, a few ghosts, and some fantasy and magic. You'll find some uncommon pets such as Katelynn, and Mr. MacCawber, and you'll find some uncommon stories, such as Patience, and Schrodinger's Other Cat.

205

You'll find stories of man's (or woman's) best friend, and stories where the animals are far from friendly. And you'll find some stories that simply refuse to fit into a category.

As always, each story in the Read on the Run series of anthologies is short, to suit your busy lifestyle.

"What an amazing find!" -- Amazon

"It was the perfect reading material for the (airplane) trip." -- Amazon

A Wink and a Smile

In this Read on the Run title, we present eighteen romances. Not love stories, although some of them do include aspects of that. But whereas love stories are often sad, each of the selections in A Wink and a Smile has either a "happily-ever-after" ending, or at least a strong suggestion that this is where the characters are heading.

That doesn't mean these tales all sound the same; to the contrary, we've found quite a diverse collection of romances. Yes, there are some traditional romances, and there's a healthy handful of budding romances, but you will also find a story set in the future, and a couple of fantasy tales. You will find stories of pastries, and candies, of young lovers and old. You will meet several matchmakers and you'll see couples reconcile, and there are even a few stories that will make you laugh.

As always, each story in the Read on the Run series of anthologies is short, to suit your busy lifestyle.

"...a charming read." -- Amazon

"I recommend this book to romance lovers and those who are busy without a lot of time to get invested in a character or a book but want to enjoy a good, warm-hearted story in the meantime." -- LibraryThing

"A Wink and a Smile is a collection of short romantic moments." -- Library Thing

Vampires, Zombies and Ghosts, Volume 1

This charming collection of short stories about vampires, zombies, ghosts, a muse, and a witch, is the first volume in this two-volume anthology in the Read on the Run series. Stories will scare you, make you laugh, and make you shed a tear or two.

Other Anthologies:

The Ancient

The Ancient is an anthology of short stories, all revolving around the notion of Aladdin's Lamp. Some of these stories use an actual lamp, some of them use a different object. But in each story, the object has some unusual magical aspect that stays with it from one person to the next. Be careful what you wish for...

"Aladdin meets the Twilight Zone." - - Amazon

A Kiss and a Promise

The six romances included in this anthology have quirky characters, or quirky locations, or quirky situations. You'll find a ghost and a new homeowner, a spaceship captain and her cartographer, a window designer and high school beau, a banker and a baker, two vampire hunters, and some supernatural beings. You'll find yourself in two different restaurants, and on another planet. You'll find deception, intrigue, and old memories. You'll find Happily-Ever-Afters, and you'll find Happy-for-Nows.

But most of all, you'll find true romance. You'll find kisses, and you'll find promises.

"Yet another delightful collection of short romantic stories!" -- Library Thing

"A cute set of stories. They are good for quick reads..." -- Library Thing

207

Novels:

The Weatherman

Josie Skye is one of the most accurate meteorologists in the country – but not everyone considers that a good thing. When weather forecasters and others start disappearing or dying and Josie fears she's one of the targets, she teams up with weather researcher, Oliver Burns, to try to find some of their missing colleagues and figure out what's going on. And what's with all these butterflies?

"Intriguing story line combined with believable characters kept my attention throughout the entire book. And when I got to the end, I was extremely disappointed that it was over! Am looking forward to the sequel....there HAS to be one!" -- Amazon

"This is an incredible ride! ... I stayed up all night reading it . . . and took a day after finishing to digest what I've read. This was, truly, a nail biter -- and you will not be let down. Pretty much throughout the book you will think you know what is happening. I won't go any further. Except to say this is a thriller indeed. " -- Goodreads

"From picking the book up to finishing it the story kept hold of me. There is mystery, death, secrets being kept, subterfuge and so much more in these pages. The story often seems straight forward until you turn the page and another spanner is thrown into the proverbial works. This story surrounding something as basic yet complex as weather will keep you turning the pages for more." -- Amazon

"The characters were likable and it has a very unique story line. I loved the surprise at the end!." -- Amazon

"Unique perspective on the topic. Left me wanting part two...... This book is science, mystery, and the lure of public opinions thrown in for good measure." -- Amazon

If you need additional information please contact us or visit our website:

E-mail: SPP@smokingpenpress.com
Website: Smokingpenpress.com

Did you enjoy reading this?
Consider posting a review on Amazon, Goodreads or wherever else you buy books, or read about books.

72477576R00125

Made in the
USA
Middletown, DE